Justin McCarthy

The Riddle Ring

A Novel: Vol.III.

Justin McCarthy

The Riddle Ring
A Novel: Vol.III.

ISBN/EAN: 9783337047221

Printed in Europe, USA, Canada, Australia, Japan

Cover: Foto ©Andreas Hilbeck / pixelio.de

More available books at **www.hansebooks.com**

THE RIDDLE RING

A NOVEL

BY

JUSTIN McCARTHY

AUTHOR OF

'DEAR LADY DISDAIN,' 'CAMIOLA,' 'THE COMET OF A SEASON,'
'DONNA QUIXOTE,' 'A FAIR SAXON,' ETC.

IN THREE VOLUMES

VOL. III.

LONDON

CHATTO & WINDUS, PICCADILLY

1896

CONTENTS OF VOL. III.

CHAPTER XIX.

'HAST THOU FOUND ME OUT, O MINE ENEMY?'

THE gallant Captain Martin paid several visits to Sir Francis Rose during the days that immediately followed the roving commission which had been given to him. Apparently, the information which he supplied to his patron was clear enough to tell Rose that the time had come when he ought to make a move, and he saw his way to the making of it.

'The other lady,' said the warlike Captain, ' will be out all the afternoon.'

'Oh! And Miss Vine?'

'Miss Vine? she will be alone.'

'Do you know anything about Mr. Conrad?'

'Mr. Conrad and Mr. Waley have an appointment together for the City at two o'clock, and their business will last them a couple of hours.'

'Good! That's all right.'

Captain Martin crouched his shoulders; he meant that for bowing.

'Did you say anything at the hotel?'

'Yes; I explained that you were a near relation of Miss Vine——'

'By marriage,' Rose interposed, with a faint smile.

'Well, I'm not quite sure that I said by marriage——'

'Doesn't matter at all.'

'No. And I said that Miss Vine would be expecting you to-day, and that you were to be shown up when you called.'

'Suppose they don't show me up when I call?'

'They will, Sir Francis.'

'Suppose they ask questions?'

'There will be no questions asked, Sir Francis.'

Captain Martin spoke in the assured tone of one who has taken all his precautions and made the way quite clear and safe.

'Good!' said Rose. 'You seem to have managed this business well, Martin.'

'I always try to manage matters well for gentlemen whom I serve, Sir Francis.'

'I know you do,' Sir Francis replied genially.

And the interview came to an end.

Sir Francis made his way to Albemarle Street, and found the hotel, and asked to be shown up to Miss Vine's sitting-room. There was no difficulty, and there were no questions asked; he was shown up at once. The attendant stopped at the door of a room on the first-floor.

'Is this Miss Vine's room?' Sir Francis asked.

' Yes, sir.'

'Then, please announce Sir Francis
Rose.'

The attendant threw the door open, and
announced in the clearest tone, 'Sir Francis
Rose,' and Rose entered and closed the
door behind him, and found himself after
a moment face to face with his wife.

The whole situation seemed to him to
be full of the deepest, or at all events the
most piquant, interest. It was a gain to
him, a new sensation to him, and therefore a joy to him, to have a moment like
that.

For the first second or so when he
entered the room he did not see Clelia.
At the farther end of the room, close to a
window, there was a solid writing-table—
not a mere lady-like trifle at all, but a good
substantial writing-table. It was rich with
ferns and flowers; behind the ferns and the
flowers Clelia sat writing.

When the announcement was made, she

sprang up from her seat, with pallid face and gleaming eyes. She kept, however, a perfect mastery of herself while the attendant was in the room. When she heard the door close she advanced a little from behind her entrenchment of ferns and flowers and desk, and confronted Rose, in agitation indeed, but undismayed.

'Hast thou found me out,' she said in thrilling Biblical language, 'O mine enemy?'

She was carried out of herself and her ordinary speech by the shock of the meeting.

'I have found you out,' Rose answered, in a voice made purposely low and pathetic; 'but I am not your enemy. I want to be your best friend.'

'Oh!' she murmured, with a shudder that really shook her whole frame.

'Why do you hate me, Clelia? I still love you.'

'Oh, for shame!' she exclaimed. 'Shame

—shame—to talk like that—after all that has passed—all that we know!'

'I still love you,' he repeated. 'Do you know that since that day—only a few days ago—when I first saw you—this time —I was fascinated by you? Yes, I was! Do you know that at first I hardly knew you, you had grown to have such an ivory-pale complexion? I never could admire what I may call a pallid-pale complexion or a sallow-pale complexion; but such an ivory-pale complexion as yours——'

'Do you think we need go on with this talk?' she asked contemptuously. 'Do you think I care what you may fancy about my complexion, or what anybody may fancy? Think of my life made miserable by you; of my youth gone in suffering through you; and then, if you will, talk to me about my complexion.'

'I am not paying you empty compliments,' he said; 'I am only telling you how I felt.'

'Very well, you like my ivory-pale complexion. You have told me that. But that, I suppose, is not all you have come here to tell me.'

'No; I have come to tell you much more.'

'Well, go on; it can all be told very shortly, can't it?'

'You are impatient, but I find no fault. It shall be told as shortly and as quickly as words can tell it. Clelia, I know how much wrong I have done you, and I want to repair it and to atone for it.'

'Listen!' she answered steadily; 'it is not a question of wrong done to me. A woman could soon forget that! God knows, we women are only too ready to forget the wrongs done us by men in whom once we trusted and whom once we loved. It is not that.'

'Then, you are willing—or, at least, not unwilling—to forgive any wrong that I may have done you? That would be a relief to my soul.'

'Oh, I am not thinking about any wrong done to me. It is over—it is gone —and I have no further concern with it.'

'Then, can we not make it up?' he asked, in a gentle and pleading voice, in the softest tone—a delicate tone which only appealed for pity, and forgiveness, and confidence.

The tone went like a sharp blade through Clelia's heart and nerves, for all its pleading sweetness and its melting soft-ness. She had heard it too often before.

'Make it up?' she exclaimed. 'As if we had merely had some trumpery quarrel over some paltry and pitiful question!'

'I have led rather a wild life,' he pleaded. 'You knew that before you married me.'

'No!' she cried. 'I never did! You took good care that I never should. You told me yourself that you had led a wandering life, and that you had been a ne'er-do-well, but that you had done nothing cruel, or mean, or wicked. Did you not tell me all that ?'

'A man in love may surely be forgiven if—when he is pressing a woman to marry him—he does not tell her all the literal truth about his past life.'

'No, he may not be forgiven! He may not be forgiven for telling falsehoods. I didn't want you to tell me the literal truth about all your past life. But you told me, again and again, that there was nothing in your past life of which a man of honour could have reason to be ashamed. And I believed you! Oh, what a fool I was to believe you! But I did—I did!'

'But you surely must have guessed at something ? You must have heard some talk in Northumberland?'

'What did I care—what would any girl have cared under such conditions—for the talk of some county families ? I had your

own assurance, and, of course, I believed it
—and that was more to me than the talk
of a dozen counties. When a girl loves a
man she believes him.'

' Then, you did love me—at that time ?'
he said, with a gleam of satisfaction in his
eyes.

' Oh yes, I loved you at that time ; you
know it well. I should not have believed
you if I had not loved you. I should not
have loved you if I had not believed you.
I thought, perhaps, you had gambled and
spent a wild life in many countries. I
fancied you had run deep into debt and set
your people against you. But I thought
that was all, and I made up my mind that
your people were unjust and ungenerous
to you—and any girl could tell you how a
woman would feel in such a case towards
a man whom she loved.'

' You believed me then.'

' I believed every word you said to
me.'

'Well, and what has changed you, after all?'

'Changed me? I am not changed! I was entrapped, and that was all. The man I married was not the man I thought I was marrying. There is the whole story. I thought I was marrying a lover, and a hero, and a gentleman, and a man of honour, and——'

'Yes—go on.'

'Is there any need for me to go on any further?'

'Yes, there is. Tell me whom you were really marrying.'

He spoke now in a deep stern tone.

'I was marrying'—and she paused and turned away from him with the contemptuous words—'I was marrying— you.'

'That defines me very well to myself, but it does not give me quite a clear idea of myself as I appear in your eyes. Tell me, Clelia—Rosita'—she contracted her

shoulders nervously at the name of Rosita
—' tell me exactly whom you married!'

'I married a man who had lived various
and shameful lives under various names in
many countries. I married a man who
had swindled widows and orphans. I
married a man who had bought his own
safety more than once by betraying his
comrades.'

'Of course, you were naturally angry
about that little affair with your mother's
money. I don't blame you. I admit that
I acted very badly about that. But I
never meant her to lose the money. I
meant to pay it back.'

'Why didn't you ask her to lend it?
She would have lent it. I could have
prevailed upon her to lend it. She would
have done it for me.'

'I managed it clumsily, I confess,' he
said thoughtfully. 'Let me see now—
what was it I did say? Oh yes: that I
knew a splendid investment — yes, I

remember—where it would be all safe and that sort of thing. That was wrong.'

'And you kept on for two years making her believe that her poor little fortune was safe and was growing.'

'Yes, yes, that was wrong; haven't I said so? But at the time I was terribly pressed for some debts—money I owed— some unlucky connections formed before our marriage.'

'Not all before our marriage.'

'Not all, perhaps, but nearly all. And, then, I wanted to keep up my character in your eyes, and to keep our home happy; and if I had not had the money things might have come out, and you would have been disappointed in me, and I did so love you.'

'I should have been far less disappointed in you if you had told me all and trusted to me,' she exclaimed. 'I was a mad girl at that time—mad, mad!—and I might have loved you and clung to you in spite of all. But why do we go on talking about all this now ? I did cling to you, even then. Did I throw you away? Did I leave you ? Or did you deliberately leave me and throw me away — yes, actually throw me away ?'

'It must have looked like that, I suppose,' he answered calmly. 'I was in one of my absurd moods, and I thought I had gone too far to be taken back on any decent terms ; and so it seemed to me at the moment the only good turn I could do for you was to get out of your sight for ever. I thought we could never be happy again, and there is something in my nature which makes me hate not to be happy.'

He spoke these last words in a reflecting sort of way, and looking at her as if he were propounding some interesting moral proposition, concerning which he expected to have her full sympathy. She listened and she looked at him. At last she said :

'I feel a sort of compassion for you—I do indeed.'

'You would—you would if you knew me,' he exclaimed with eagerness. 'I sometimes feel a compassion for myself.'

'Ah yes; that I can quite understand. I do know you—I know you only too well. You always seem to me now like a man who was born without a conscience, even more than that—like a man who was born without a soul.'

'Do you know,' he said, quite seriously, 'I have sometimes thought the same thing about myself. I have sometimes thought that I have no soul; but can there be such a thing? Of course, all sorts of materialists say that we none of us have any souls, and on that point I am not qualified to express any dogmatic opinion. But would it be possible for one man to have no soul while all other people, or, at all events, most other people, had souls? That seems to me unlikely, and yet it has often occurred to me as if it must have happened in my case. Because I never feel really sorry for anything, or responsible about anything.'

'Well,' Clelia said sadly, after a pause, 'it is of no use our talking about these things—at least, I mean it is of no use our arguing about them. We see everything from such a different point of view. I could not live with you again. You have no sense of right and wrong.'

'Oh, come ! what is right, and what is wrong ?'

'When I had become convinced of that by bitter and cruel experience,' she said, unheeding his interruption, 'I felt that my life was a failure, and that we could never indeed, as you have said, be happy again. Still, I clung to you, and I hoped against hope. Then you threw me off, and after that my heart became as adamant. Yes, it did !'

'Threw you off ! Well, is not that rather a harsh expression ?'

'Call it by any name you like.'

'You mean when I sent you that ring?'

'When you sent me that ring, with the engraved message—that message of mock tragic farewell which it conveyed.'

'I thought it only fair. I was making a fool of myself at the time. I had fallen terribly in love with a woman who was not really fit to tie your shoe-strings, and I thought it was only right to give you a hint that way. Apropos, where is the ring? Have you got it?'

'No, I have not.'

'What has become of it?'

'I flung it away. I flung it from me in the Bois de Boulogne, near the railings where I gave it to you, where you gave me that other ring—near the place where we first met long before.'

'Was it not rather imprudent to throw the ring away in such a public place? Somebody might pick it up.'

'I didn't care about that, so long as I was rid of it.'

'It might spell out a story.'

'What did I care then whether it did or not ? What do I care now ? Can you not understand my misery and my madness ? Nothing could alter the story, let who will spell it out.'

'Well,' he said slowly, as if he were thinking over some new proposition in social science, 'I suppose women never look at these things quite as men do.'

'I suppose not. I hope not—if men in general look at them as you do. But they don't—I know they don't.'

'Indeed ; has anyone been trying to teach you ? Don't believe him; he is sure to be only a humbug.'

She paid no attention to this remark, or, rather, she simply tossed it from her.

'You have not told me yet,' she said, 'why you came here, or how you found me out.'

'I came to do my best to make up matters between us.'

'Make up matters! Do you think it is a commonplace quarrel about some trumpery difference of opinion?'

'No, no. I don't say that; but I do say that there is no reason why we should not be content with each other, and be together again. Listen to me, Rosita.'

'Oh, please don't use that name again!'

'I'll use any name that pleases you,' he said sternly; 'Clelia, Lady Rose—anything you will—my wife, if you will put up with that. I have come to tell you something.'

'Tell it to me, and then go away and leave me with my misery.'

'I have not come to leave you with your misery. I have come to take you from your misery. I have come to make you happy.'

'Oh!' she groaned.

' Yes, I have—if only you will consent to act like a sensible woman.'

' Well, tell me what a sensible woman ought to do. I shall listen.'

' Why, of course, she ought to take back her husband when he comes to her repentant, and confesses his errors, and simply pleads for pardon and for pity. Listen, Rosita, my wife. I have come here because I love you ; because the very moment I saw you the other day I fell in love with you again—all over again. I said to my soul, " Why did I ever fail to appreciate that divine woman ?" I did indeed ; I did, on my honour. " How could I have allowed myself to be fooled away from her by any idle illusions of my own ?" I only want to be redeemed and regenerated. Take me ; redeem me ; re-generate me.'

His voice sounded exquisitely in its pleading cadence. Francis Rose knew its fascination. For the moment he felt divinely happy. He delighted in his power of stage-play. There was an entire novelty about the situation which positively fascinated him.

'Heaven knows,' she said sorrowfully, 'that if I believed I could do any good for you I would try to do it, even at the utter sacrifice of myself. But, oh! I know it is all of no use. It amuses you now to play this part. When once this had been played, and played successfully, you would want to be amused by trying some quite different part. We both know—you and I perfectly well know—that we could not make life happy or even endurable for each other. Ah, no! Gone is gone; dead is dead.'

'I am in love with you,' he declared, 'as I never was before, and you must come with me.'

'So far as my own feelings are concerned,' she said, 'you know that I would rather go into the Thames than return to

you. But I can't throw myself into the
Thames, because I can't commit such a
crime. I suppose I was sent into the
world for some purpose, and I must stay
here until I am ordered away. But so far
as my own feelings are concerned, I should
welcome the river as a relief.'

'You were always poetic,' he declared
admiringly. 'You were always a curious
mixture of poetry and religion. I used to
think that the two didn't often go together.
I fancied that if a woman was very poetic
that meant the longing to dash herself
against the bars of the cage—to try to
break bounds, kick over the traces, and all
that. But you were always so religious
and self-restrained. I used to wonder at
it, and I used to admire it, too, sometimes.
But I tell you straight out that I did not
properly appreciate you. Oh yes. I have
not the slightest hesitation in admitting
that. Now I see things quite differently,
and I see what a fool I was not to have

understood better, and I am madly in love
with you again. Again? Oh, more than
ever! Come, Clelia; I am not lost past
redemption. Give me another chance!
You will not be sorry for it; you will find
that I am not altogether undeserving—you
will indeed.'

'Merciful Heaven!' she murmured in
an agony of perplexity. 'If I could only
believe that there was anything true in all
this!'

'You can believe it; you must believe
it; you shall believe it!'

He made a movement towards her. She
drew back from him.

'One moment,' she said. 'Frank'—for
the first time she called him by his name,
and a thrill of pride and joy passed through
him as he heard the word.

'By Jove! I have triumphed,' he
thought, and his eyes lighted with all the
fire of success.

Her heart, indeed, was melting towards

him, and not so much towards him as towards the possible thought that she might yet help to make him happy; to make him a better man—to redeem him, as he put it himself. And yet it seemed as if she could not trust him. She had been deceived so often before.

'Frank,' she said again, 'I don't want to bring up old stories; it would be of no use to either of us to go over such things. But I do know that many of your troubles——'

'You may call them by a harsher name,' he said in a submissive tone, 'if you like.'

'Why should I? What good would that do? Well, what I was going to say was this : you suffered much from want of money——'

'Yes, didn't I? I loved to be happy, and to make people happy——'

'Well, well,' she broke in rather impatiently, because somehow that was not exactly the impression of his nature which remained upon her mind. 'What I was going to say was this.'

She seemed to have great difficulty in saying it. She looked at the carpet, she glanced up to the ceiling; her struggling voice would not come.

Francis Rose listened with eagerness and wondering expectancy.

'I was very poor,' she began, and then she stopped again.

'What did that matter to me?' he asked heroically, still very eager. 'I knew you were poor when I asked you to be my wife.'—'What is coming?' he wondered. 'These women are so odd.'

'Yes; but men don't always quite appreciate the sacrifice they are going to make.' She could not help remembering how often her want of money had been flung in her face—how often her husband had told her that she was under an immense obligation to him for having condescended to marry 'a

beggar-girl.' Her face almost crimsoned
for a moment, but she resolutely put all
such thoughts away. 'What I want to
say is this,' she went on : ' I am not poor
now. A kind and dear friend whom I
have lost'—and the tears came into her eyes
at the thought—' has divided her fortune
between her daughter and me. It was a
large fortune undivided. It is a large
fortune for me. It is riches for me when
I take my share. I did not want it, but
they would insist on it.' Half uncon-
sciously she turned her eyes upon his face
and studied his expression. Had he been
less self-controlled, less skilled in moulding
the mask of his face, she might have found
him out once more. But, utterly surprised
as he was, wildly delighted as he was, eager
for a reconciliation as he was, he did not
allow any gleam of joy to light up under
his pince-nez. He only said :

'I am glad, if it will help to make you
happy ; but I am not thinking of your

money—I am thinking of yourself.' 'I
wonder how will that do?' he thought at
that critical moment.

'What I want to say is this,' she began
once again with what she wanted to say.
'I want to say that I should like you to
share—the money with me. Oh, I should
be so glad to give it! It might make you
happy; and there would be enough—far
more than enough—for me; and even to
leave me with the means of doing some
good if it came in my way.'

'Thank you,' he said quite coldly. 'I
ask you for your love, and you offer me
half your money——'

'Oh, as much as you like—as much as
you will have,' she interrupted.

'Thank you again. I ask for bread, and
you give me a stone! I want you. I
claim your forgiveness, and—well—your
love; and you offer to divide your money
with me! Thank you, Lady Rose; no, I
don't want your money. I have enough

for myself. I have come in for what property there is in the old place, and as I have never hitherto had much to do with it, it has not been particularly encumbered, and I propose to live a life worthy of a man who is head of the house of the Northumbrian Roses. I shall live like a gentleman again, as my ancestors did—as I might have done myself if it had not been for want of money and too much temptation. I am glad to hear that you are well cared for, Rosita ; but I did not come to talk about your money. I came to talk about yourself and your love. Come, Rosita, do try to understand that years and trials and ill-luck—yes, and lately good luck—may alter a man ! Responsibility alters a man. I am now the head of my house.'

A sudden outburst of passion flamed through her. Something in his melodramatic tone shocked her. She could not believe in him. She was furious with herself for having gone even for a moment near to believing in him.

'Responsibility will not alter you !' she exclaimed vehemently ; and he drew back surprised for the moment at her unexpected display of fierce emotion. 'You will never be anything other than what you were and what you are. You are play-acting at this very moment——'

'So I am, by Jove !' he thought to himself. 'How confoundedly clever she is !'

'Play-acting, play-acting ! There was never any reality about you for good or ill; there was never any real Francis Rose— but only a play-actor and a mummer !'

He drew back as if he had been struck in the face.

'No more play-acting and mumming, my lady,' he said in a stern voice. 'You shall find that I am terribly in earnest this time. I'll conquer you ! I'll tame you— take my word for that !'

'You'll never make me care for
you——'

'I don't mind about that ; I'll bring
you to your knees before me——'

She made a scornful gesture.

'Yes, I will. You shall be my wife
again.'

'Never !' she said more gently—more
gently perhaps because her mind was all
made up by this time.

'Just wait and see. I'll pass you under
the yoke. I'll be a kind husband to you ;
but there shall be no petticoat government
in my house ! You shall shed many a tear
for this ; but I'll make a good wife of you.
So I bid you good-bye for the present; but
I'll come again when, where, and how you
least expect.'

'Stay a moment,' she said quietly,
although with trembling lips and limbs.
'Once again I make you my offer : you
shall have as much of my money as you
like to take.'

'Thank you. I shall have you and your money, both, when I choose to take them.'

'You forget,' she said contemptuously, 'that we are living in a civilized country. There are laws in England to protect even women.'

'Not to protect mutinous wives,' he said, with a mocking laugh, as he was turning to go.

'One can leave England,' she said.

'You can leave England,' he replied, 'but you cannot leave me. You can't shake me off now that I am in love with you again, and am determined that you shall be my wife again. I have ways of finding out things, and I shall find you out wherever you go and wherever you are. Good-bye for the moment. We shall meet again soon.'

Then, with a manner once more composed, he left her.

She sat down and covered her face with

her hands, and the immediate strain being relaxed, she found her woman's relief in a burst of tears. She was glad he could not see her then.

CHAPTER XX.

SIR FRANCIS dined alone that evening at the Voyagers' Club. He avoided seeing Conrad or anyone ; he wanted to be alone for a time at least, and to think things over. All the day he had been treading on air. It seemed to him as if he must have a sort of halo of happiness round his head. He felt supremely happy ; he had a cluster of new sensations with which to make his life very well worth living. The determination to recapture his wife was a positive delight to him.

'She shall fall in love with me yet—by Jove ! she shall. I'll woo her as the lion wooes his bride. She'll think all the better of me for it. I understand a woman like that. How her eyes flashed! By Jove! what a triumph to recapture such a woman!'

All this he kept saying to himself and thinking over and over again. What a woman to sit at the head of one's table and entertain with, he thought; for he had got a new ambition now. He had long been a social outlaw; now he yearned, above all things, to reconquer West End society. He had voluntarily dragged his name and his family down into the dust in many countries; but all the time he had been vain of his birth, even while, with deliberate cynicism, he degraded and debased it. For he was, as Clelia had said, and as he admitted frankly to himself when she said it, always a play-actor. He was always playing a part; he had played the part of the betrayer more for the sake of playing the part than for the sensuous pleasure of the betrayal; he had played the

part of the loving husband, and he had
played the part of the cynical, brutal
husband ; now it would be his happiness to
be a leader of society, with a charming
wife to manage things for him.

' That's how we do it !' he said to himself exultingly, in the slang of our day.

But after he had dined he felt that he
wanted to talk over the whole subject, and
there was nobody with whom he could
talk it over freely except the faithful
Waley. Moreover, he had certain ideas,
at present only seething in his head, which
he hoped that the faithful Waley might
help him to put into bodily shape, and
even into bodily action.

So he sent a messenger to the faithful
Waley's lodgings to ask Waley to come to
him as quickly as he could. He knew
that Waley's habits were methodical, and
that after ten or half-past ten at night he
might be counted on until any hour of the
morning.

About eleven o'clock Sir Francis was smoking in the quiet recess which has been more than once described in this story, and, if we may say so, in another story as well.

Then Mr. Waley quietly appeared upon the scene.

' Just got your message, chief, and so I came along.'

' All right, Waley; glad to see you.'

' Nothing very serious, I hope ?' Waley asked anxiously.

Sir Francis looked upstairs and downstairs. There was nobody near ; save for the reading-rooms and smoking-rooms, the club was empty.

' Waley, I have made a fool of myself !'

' What, again ?' Waley asked, with a broad grin.

' Yes, again. No, by Jove! I don't think I have, but I was very near doing it—I all but did it ; and then it turns out that I didn't, after all. Look here, Waley : I've struck ile again.'

'You generally do strike ile,' Waley said, 'wherever you strike at all ; so I'm not much surprised. But would you mind telling us a little about it ?'

'Yes, of course I'll tell you—first of all, how I was near making a fool of myself. Waley, I have seen my wife !'

'Not really ?' Waley asked, with a manner of comparative indifference.

'Yes, I did ! I saw her for the first time a few days ago ; I mean, of course, for the first time since we fell out— separated—all that, you know.'

'Yes, I hold on to your meaning. Go ahead.'

'Well, I saw her by chance a few days ago. Did I tell you ? No ? I dare say I meant to tell you, but I forgot all about it.'

'All right,' Waley observed, not caring much either way.

' Waley, I saw her again to-day !'

' Did you really ?   Well ?'

' Well, listen to me, Waley. I have fallen madly in love with her !'

' Oh, come now,' Waley protested.

' Yes, but I have, though. I can't imagine how I ever came to think that stupid little brute of a girl could be worth causing her a moment's pain ! I am madly in love with her, Waley—only fancy ! madly in love with my own wife ! What do you think of that ?'

' Does seem odd, don't it ?' Waley asked, not, however, without a smile of something like gratification expanding over his not unhandsome face.

' Yes ; she is bewitching—she is divine ! I can't tell you how I felt at meeting her again !'

' I know how I should feel if I were to meet my wife again,' Waley said ; ' and I rather think I know how she would feel, too !'

'Yes; but, then, your wife, my excellent Waley, was no doubt a worthy and deserving woman, but mine is a goddess.'

'Half a second, please. Some time in finding it out, weren't you?'

'I was, Waley! We are strange beings —some of us! I did not know that I had loved her so much——'

'No; I never heard you say so at any time before——'

'How could I say it, Waley? I didn't know it myself——'

'Ah yes, there it is, you see! Still, I'm pleased that you have found it out at last. But I don't see how you have made a fool of yourself unless you propose to give up everything else, and tie yourself on to your wife's petticoat-tail like somebody in the play—Antony, wasn't it? No, I believe she wasn't quite exactly his wife; but the notion is the same, don't you know.'

'How I was near making a fool of myself was this,' Rose answered gravely and slowly. 'I fell so suddenly dead in love with her that I begged and prayed of her to take me back again—yes, I did! And I thought all the time that she hadn't a penny of money! You know my way— it was a thrilling sensation to me, the thought of capturing her again—and she might have had me back to her there as she stood!'

'For how long?' Waley curtly asked.

'For how long? Oh, well, that is not quite to the point. Still, judging by my present sensations, I should say for ever and ever——'

'Present sensations!' Waley interposed, with the accent on the 'present.'

'My excellent good Waley, who can know about the sensations of the future? Have we the divine gift of prophecy, you and I?'

'About some things, I almost think I have,' Waley said, with a twinkle in his eye.

' Oh, but come, look here—we are rather wandering away from the point. This is how I was near making a fool of myself. Now let us see how, after all, I didn't.'

' Yes, I rather want to come to that.'

' There is an absence of the poetic about you, Waley, which I sometimes am inclined to deplore.'

' Oh, Lord! there is an absence of all sorts of good things about me which somebody is always deploring. I have heard my wife make many a deploring of that kind, and I dare say she was quite right, poor old dear!'

' She was quite right,' Rose said decisively. ' But we were not talking about her. We were talking about my being very near to making a fool of myself, and not making a fool of myself, after all.'

' Right you are.'

' Well, here it is. My wife is an heiress, and I never knew it until to-day.'

'By Jove! you don't meant that?' Mr. Waley exclaimed, with a suddenly kindling interest.

'Yes, she is indeed! She has been left a whole lot of money, and she offered to give me half of it, or more than half if I liked.'

'Come! that is good business,' Waley declared, with lighting eyes; 'and you take it, of course?'

'Take it, my dear Waley? How little you understand such a woman as that.'

'Well, but tell us——'

'Why, of course, I rejected it with a lofty disdain.'

'Well, I never!'

'Don't you see that that is the very way to charm a woman like that?'

'You see, I haven't had the pleasure of knowing her.'

'You may take her on my description. That is the very way to get her back. I mounted the high horse—the heroic horse

—at once! I declared that I scorned her
money, and that I only wanted her love.
And see here, Waley, I'll have both. I
am madly in love with her! I want her
money—of course I want her money—but
I am in love with her as I never was
before. She must come back to me.
Waley, if she does not consent, I'll carry
her off by force! I will! You shall
help me, Waley!'

'Oh! I'll help you in anything fast
enough; and, of course, the wife belongs
to her husband, and he may carry her off
whenever he likes. I suppose that's as
good law as they make. But I don't
think we often hear of husbands carrying
off their own wives much in our day—I
mean, when the husbands have already
dropped the good ladies down for a con-
siderable time.'

'Well, if she won't come by smooth
ways she shall by rough! If she won't
come by fair ways she shall by foul! Do

you know, Waley, I feel already thrilled
by this new sensation ! It makes life
worth living. I was just beginning to
find life growing a little dull and mono-
tonous. My life was getting to be as
colourless as a subterranean stream——'

' I've been in the Mammoth Cave in
Kentucky,' Mr. Waley interjected, with
what seemed to him sufficient appositeness.
' The fishes there are all blind, because
they don't want any eyes. What would
be the good of eyes where they couldn't
see ?'

' I want eyes,' Sir Francis exclaimed
enthusiastically, ' if only to look on her !
Waley, you shall see her !'

' Delighted, I am sure.'

' I am afraid you don't think me quite in
earnest, Waley. But I am—this time I am.
I shall have her back, and then, of course,
I shall have the money, too. What a
wonderful stroke of luck ! I wasn't thinking about money, I was only in love with

her, and suddenly she turns round and offers me half of her fortune, or more if I want it. Waley, don't you think it is enough to make a man believe in what we read, in good books, you know, about conjugal love, and virtue, and all that? Doesn't it really seem as if virtue was to be rewarded in my own case? I fell in love with my wife—absolutely fell in love with her—with my own wife—and for her own sake absolutely, absolutely for her own sake! Well, a man ought to fall in love with his wife, ought he not?'

'If he hasn't done it before, yes, certainly,' Waley said, in the tone of an oracle.

'Or if, having once fallen in love with her before, he has somehow happened to fall out of love with her, is it not his duty to fall in love with her again?'

'Half a second, Sir Francis;' and the right thumb and forefinger came together. 'I am not much of an authority on

people's duties, but I should say it certainly was,' Waley answered somewhat
grimly.

He was not overjoyed at the appearance
of a woman on their somewhat venturous
and enterprising stage. He did not want
the chief to become too soft-hearted and
domestic, and yet he had always had an
uneasy consciousness that somehow the
chief's wife had not been altogether well
treated.

'Well, then, you see, I was fulfilling
my duty all because of love, and here is
the reward of the fulfilment of duty! Do
you know, Waley, it ought to be enough
to give a man a new impulse towards the
good. It might inspire one towards the
leading of a better life.'

'What, the chance of getting the
money?'

'No, no! how can you be so material?
The fact that the chance of getting the
money came after the resolve to win back

her love. Don't you see, Waley? Good
heavens, man! how can you be so dull
as not to see?'

'I'm a dull man naturally,' Waley said,
with a broad, good-humoured smile. 'I
can't help myself. Nature made me.'

'Nature didn't make you dull; you
are not dull—you are nothing of the
kind. You can get at an idea often much
quicker than I can. How can you be so
dull in this case? Look here, I'll go
over it all again. I have neglected my
wife. I have deserted her. Good——'

'Bad, I should call it,' said the prosaic
Waley.

'Yes, yes; in that sense I admit, of
course. But, then, take what comes next.
I repent, I determine to reform, I seek
out my wife, I tell her I am sorry for
what I have done, I tell her I am in love
with her more than ever; I ask her to
forgive me, to take me back, to reform
me, to regenerate me; and then I find

out, to my utter surprise, that she has a
lot of money about which I never heard!
Does that not strike you, Waley, as if
virtue were really made its own reward,
as if the powers above had marked out
my future for me?'

'I am afraid I don't see it—quite.'

'My dear Waley, I am afraid you are
rather a sceptic.'

'Don't think I altogether know what
a sceptic is; but in this case I suppose
the young woman would have come in
for the fortune whether you had fallen in
love with her again or not.'

'You don't understand me,' Sir Francis
said, in a tone of disappointed feeling.
'I suppose it would be of no use my
trying to make you understand me on a
question like that.'

'We generally understand each other
pretty well — don't we, chief?' Waley
asked in a somewhat puzzled and almost
querulous voice.

'We do—we do; but on points of feeling, the higher sentiments, perhaps we
don't always quite hit it off——'

'Oh, very like,' interrupted the downright Waley. 'I'm not much on the
higher sentiments. But just tell me what
you mean to do, and how I can help you,
and I'll do all I can.'

'But I haven't quite thought it out
yet, Waley. I don't quite see my way
yet. You see,' he added somewhat fret-
fully, 'I generally get hold of an idea
myself, and then I pass it on to you to
work it into action for me. But I
can't well do that in this case, can I,
Waley?'

'Oh, by Jupiter, no!' Waley promptly
replied. 'I haven't the least idea of
what ought to be done in this case.
When it comes to a question between
husband and wife, then I'm about the
worst chap in the world to be able to
give advice that's worth the having.'

'Well, I must think it over,' Sir Francis said, somewhat tartly.

He had got the idea into his head that there was a faint note of mutiny or of something approaching to it in Waley's voice. He did not like that. He had been for a long time accustomed to rely on Waley's promptings in everything. He had always relied implicitly and unquestioningly on himself to find out what he wanted to have done ; but he had always relied on Waley to suggest the way by which the object might be gained or the enterprise worked out. Now that he had set his heart upon this new enterprise, he found nothing suggestive, or even responsive, about Waley's tone and manner.

There was a certain artistic or æsthetic —æsthetic in the old sense of the word— sensitiveness in Rose's nature and nerves that often enabled him to scent out from far off the evidences of a coming danger as 'the leaves of the shrinking mimosa' are said to feel far in advance the tramp of the horses' feet on the prairie.

So now Rose appeared to foretell the coming of a crisis, when Waley would not work with him quite as cordially as he had always worked before. He had known that Waley had a strong objection to the intrusion of a woman into any of the common enterprises of himself and his chief. But he had known, too—and it was of much greater importance to him now — that despite Waley's quarrel with his own wife, and his separation from her, and his relief at getting rid of her, there was a curious vein of compassionate tenderness to women deep down in Waley's odd nature, and that he would be likely enough to insist that men must play the straight game with women, whatever they did.

Rose told himself again and again—was telling himself as he sat there talking with Waley — that he meant to play the

straightest game with Clelia Rose that ever
could be played. He simply meant to
make his wife—his own lawful wife—fall
in love with him again, and come back to
him again. There was nothing in his
proposal, in his enterprise, of which pale-
lipped morality itself could disapprove.
On the contrary, it was the very thing
which the palest-lipped morality ought to
go earnestly in for. Now, as Rose well
knew, his devoted Waley did not by any
means go in for pale-lipped morality. On
the contrary, Waley had done, or sanc-
tioned, many things over which—to use
Carlyle's phrase—'moralities not a few
must shriek aloud.' But, still, Rose had
always been conscious in an oblique kind
of way that there were sentimental weak-
nesses in Waley of which he himself could
render no account to his conscience.

When Rose wanted a thing done for his
own purpose, that purpose became the
guide of his conscience; other guiding

light he had none, and wanted none. But he had noticed in his faithful henchman a sort of conscience which naturally and at the first modelled itself on the conscience of the chief, and yet which might possibly be roused into vague doubt, and then into downright question.

Sir Francis Rose felt towards Waley this night—he could not quite tell why—a little in the mood of Shakespeare's King Richard towards Buckingham when he makes a secret proposal, and meets with no genial response. 'Tut, tut, thou art all ice—thy kindness freezes!' Sir Francis Rose thought the kindness of Waley was somewhat frozen that night, and the idea gave him food for contemplation. Perhaps he was wrong, he said to himself. Waley was very friendly and comrade-like, but his kindness did somehow seem to freeze.

CHAPTER XXI.

'WHY SUMMON HIM—AND TRUST NOT ME?'

THE faithful Waley was looking out of the windows of the red flat near Berkeley Square one evening about seven, a few nights after the evening when we saw him last. He was somewhat puzzled in mood. He had not been quite able to account for the manner of the chief these few days past. He did not by any means approve of the 'petticoat interest' which to all appearance the chief had lately been determined to import into the dramatic fiction of the lives of the little confederacy.

Waley had a sort of superstition on the

subject. It amounted to this : They three,
Sir Francis, Waley himself, and Marmaduke Coffin—poor, good, absurd old Coffin !
—had all been equally unlucky in their
married lives. No flitch of bacon could
be won by any of them in any conceivable
Dunmow festival. Why, then, transport
the ill-luck along with them? Why take
up with it again voluntarily and unsought?
Why run out of one's way to get hold of
it? Waley had probably never heard of
Hogarth's sign representing 'The Man
loaded with Mischief,' which used to
hang in Oxford Street up to quite recent
years. The Man loaded with Mischief
had his wife seated on his shoulders. To
Mr. Waley's mind, a man was loaded with
mischief who had his wife or any other
woman on his shoulders.

Suddenly a cab stopped at the door, and
Marmaduke Coffin stepped cautiously out.
There was a dispute about the cab-fare,
and then Coffin crossed the pavement.

He glanced quickly, quietly, either way before he rang the bell at the door.

There was something very peculiar about the walk of Mr. Marmaduke Coffin. The front of the foot—the toes—seemed to take a sudden and strong grip of the earth. They held on to it, and relaxed the grip but slowly and cautiously. No matter how quick the pace of the moving man, the same peculiarity could be noticed in the movement. That is, it could be noticed by anybody who had an eye for noticing anything. Nine out of every ten people have not such an eye. To them nothing is peculiar—it is all as by lot, God wot. But anybody who had an eye a little better instructed would have noticed the peculiar movement of Mr. Marmaduke Coffin's walk.

The same peculiarity might be traced in the movement of the beasts whom the noble savage pursues, and in the movement of the noble savage himself. The instinct in each case is that of not going too far in either direction to be able to turn and wind with a single throb and impulse of will. Put as much force as you fairly can on the impulse; but, all the same, catch the earth, and grip it so that you may be ready to turn and wind at any moment with all your full strength, all your full speed. That is really the foundation and secret of this peculiarity of movement. It was a secret which showed itself in the step of Marmaduke Coffin. But it made no impression whatever on the unimaginative and uninquiring mind of Mr. Albert Edward Waley. Mr. Waley had not many friendships, but when he did make a friendship he generally took it for granted.

Waley himself promptly opened the door of the flat.

'Hello, my noble sportsman!' Waley exclaimed. 'So you have come over, have you?'

'Did you expect that I was not going to come over, Mr. Waley?' Coffin mildly asked.

'Oh no, Coffin; I knew you would come, old boy, and that was only my way of welcoming you—see?'

'I am sure you meant it well, Mr. Waley.'

'Why, of course I did, Coffin. What else on earth should I have meant it for? But now that you have come, do you know what you have come for?'

'No, I don't, Mr. Waley; but I make no doubt you can tell me.'

'I? Not a bit of it, old man. But you really don't know?'

'I don't know anything. I got your letter——'

'Yes, yes, of course.'

'And then I came.'

'And then you came — and that's all?'

'That's all, Mr. Waley. I wait for

further details, as they say in the newspapers.'

' Do they ?' Mr. Waley asked somewhat
distractedly.   ' I hadn't noticed.'

' Do they—what ?' Mr. Coffin asked,
a little out of tune with the latest question.

' Oh, well '—Mr. Waley pulled himself
a little together—' I wasn't quite thinking
of what the newspapers say, or about the
further details they may find it necessary
to wait for.   What I wanted to ask was
whether the chief hadn't given you any
hint about the business for which he
brought you over here ?'

' No, Mr. Waley ; I didn't ask him any
questions.'

' Why, of course you did not,' Waley
exclaimed earnestly.   ' He knows what is
best ; he knows what he wants done.   I
don't ask him any questions, I can tell
you.   But I thought perhaps he might
have let you know what he was bringing

you over to London for, and told you to
tell me.'

' No, Mr. Waley,' Coffin answered, with
all the quietude of self-conscious honesty ;
' he told me nothing at all.'

' And he didn't even tell you to ask
me ?'

' No, Mr. Waley, he didn't.'

' All right,' Waley said, in restored good
spirits ; ' he'll tell me when the right time
comes. He said that he would, and of
course he will.'

Marmaduke Coffin let his eyes fall on
the carpet as he heard these words from
Mr. Waley. It had appeared to his
mind as if he must have been summoned
over from Paris to London on some
very peculiar business. He had certainly
counted when he came over on finding
Waley in the full secret, and on receiving
instructions from him ; but it did not
take him long to get hold of the fact
that he was brought over to London for

business which, so far at least, had been
kept out of the knowledge of Albert
Edward Waley. This was to him like
a note of coming promotion. We all
know what a trouble it is when any
service is clogged by a lack of promotion.
We have had to make rules about this
in the army and the Civil Service of our
country, by virtue of which some of the
grandest triumphs that were accomplished
for the State in other days could not
be accomplished for the State in our
days.

This we call progress. Now, there
were no such rules, to be sure, in the
service to which Mr. Marmaduke Coffin
had devoted himself, and he well knew
that he might go on until the age of
ninety-five, should he live so long, without receiving any promotion, if any other
man could do the work he was wanted
for better than he could. So he felt a
thrill of pride and hope and joy when

he heard that he had been called over from Paris to undertake some business about which as yet Mr. Waley had not even been consulted. Mr. Waley, on the other hand, felt a little put out by the fact that he had not been consulted, but his loyal heart was easily satisfied by the assurance that he would be allowed to know in good time, and that it would all come out right.

There was a silence for some seconds. Then Coffin spoke in his laconic, mono-syllabic sort of way.

'Chief not in?'

'No, he's not in now; if he were, I shouldn't have kept you waiting all this time, Coffin, old boy.'

'In—when?'

'He didn't say, my sententious youth. Didn't say a word to me about expecting you this morning, or waiting in for you; but I think you had better wait a little here. I think he is dining with some chaps at the Voyagers', and it's very likely he'll want to see you later on.'

'Thank you, Mr. Waley, I'll wait. My time is his.'

'All right, old man ; so is mine. Well, tell me all the news from Paris. Not the fashionable news, Coffin. I know you ain't just the sort of man to take an interest in the news that would suit the *Ladies' Pictorial.*'

Just at that moment the sharp ring of a telegraph messenger was heard at the door. Waley jumped up.

'Excuse me a moment, Coffin,' he said breathlessly. 'I always like to take in these messages myself when I get the chance.'

'Right,' said the sententious Coffin.

In a moment Waley was back, looking a little crestfallen.

'It's a telegram for you, Coffin,' he said blankly.

Coffin took it and opened it with his

usual air of melancholy indifference to events of life, strokes of fate, sudden in-rushes of good luck, and all the rest.

'Chief wants me at the Voyagers' at ten-thirty,' he said concisely.

'Oh, he does; all right,' Waley murmured.

'Then, I needn't wait here any longer?' Coffin asked.

'Don't see any necessity. Don't give yourself up too much to the pleasures of the capital, Coffin. You are a rare old boy, I know, for the pleasures of the capital.'

'I'll go and get shaved,' said Coffin. 'Some of the shops in Bond Street don't close until eight. Just half-past seven now.'

'Until ten-thirty your time is your own,' Waley said. 'Use it, and don't abuse it, old chap.'

'Thanks,' Coffin replied; and he vanished from the room with his peculiar tread—

the movement of one who felt that he might find enemies and dangers and pitfalls and snares anywhere along his way.

'Rum chap, Coffin!' Waley murmured to himself. 'Wonder if he really likes anyone? Think he does like the chief. Don't think he likes me. Wonder if he hates most people, and would do them an ill turn—or is it only his manner? People have such odd sorts of manners sometimes.'

His reflections were cut short by hearing a latchkey turn in the front-door. The chief, he thought. He must have met Coffin on the stairs.

Sir Francis Rose came in. He was not looking quite so bright and airy as usual. A shade of embarrassment, and even of sombreness, was over him. He saluted Waley with an air of indifference.

'Ho, Waley!' was all he said.

'You expected me, chief, didn't you?' Waley asked.

'Expected you? Oh yes; of course I did.'

'Did you meet Coffin? He has been here.'

The chief contracted his eyebrows, and a curious light flashed from under them.

'Yes; I met Coffin. It's all right,' he replied.

'You don't want me just now?'

Waley rose to his feet.

'Just now? Yes, I do. I have time enough yet. Sit down.'

The obedient Waley sat down, and waited silently for the next words of his chief.

'Look here, Waley: you must get this young fellow off as fast as possible to Patagonia, or somewhere else. The sooner the better.'

'What young fellow?' Waley asked in some surprise.

They had not been talking of any young fellow. It has been already mentioned

more than once that Mr. Waley's many
excellent qualities did not include much
imaginative faculty, or much gift of what
may be called dramatic insight into the
feelings and the preoccupations of the
minds of other human beings. He had
not for the moment the slightest idea ot
what his chief was thinking or talking
about.

'This young fellow, Jim Conrad. He
is rather in the way here just now, and I
want him out of the way.'

'Oh,' Mr. Waley said reflectively; 'I
dare say that will be easy enough.'

'All right. I am very glad.'

'Yes; that ought to be easy work. My
idea is that he will be only too glad to get
away anywhere, and the farther away the
better.'

'Good,' Sir Francis said, turning in his
chair contentedly. 'Then, get him away,
Waley, there's a good chap.'

'Fact is,' Waley said confidently, 'there's

something wrong with the poor lad. I
fancy it must be the old story.'

'What old story ?'

'Well, isn't there something that people
always say about *cherchez la femme*?'

'Yes. How is that ? What do you
mean ?' Rose asked sharply, and with
suddenly-contracting eyebrows.

'I have long had it in my mind,' Waley
answered slowly and gravely, 'that some
woman is at the bottom of the whole
affair. He is in love with some girl who
won't have him or can't have him, and he
wants to go away anywhere out of the
whole business. When a young chap like
that is crossed in love, he always wants to
go away somewhere out of civilization.
Lord bless you! I have been like that myself in my younger days. You don't know
much about it, chief, I dare say, for the
women have generally done the love-
making for you. But I can see his case
with half an eye.'

Rose looked keenly again at Waley. Could it possibly be that Waley knew anything or suspected anything of the real state of affairs? But Waley's expression was one of utter simplicity and innocence.

'Odd thing!' Mr. Waley went on in a sort of philosophical study of life and the ways of men. 'Odd phrase that, being crossed in love! Now, I have long been of opinion that the real cross in love is where the girl is willing to have you. By Jove! what becomes of the love then? How soon it all melts away! But he don't think that just now, bless you! Yes; I fancy I shall not have much difficulty in getting him off to Patagonia.'

Sir Francis flung himself back in his chair. Every word that Waley was saying made him only the more convinced that Conrad would not go to Patagonia just now. He felt a passion of hatred and jealousy rising in his mind against Jim Conrad. But it would have been an un-

speakable torture to his vanity and his
self-love to know that Waley suspected
anything of the feelings that were thrilling
through his heart. To Waley he must
always seem the conquering hero among
women—the irresistible Don Juan—the
wrecker of female hearts. It would be a
pitiful come-down for him if his devoted
follower were to find out that Sir Francis
Rose could be jealous of any man—especially on account of Sir Francis Rose's own
wife. He hastened to assume a tone of
less keen interest in the matter.

'Well, get him away as soon as you can,
Waley. Of course, I need not tell you to
make-good use of him. He might be
made of great service to us in some business or other.'

'Oh, you trust me to turn him to good
account. He's a clever young fellow, and
a plucky young fellow, and we'll put him
on for all he's worth—you may depend
upon that.'

'I can depend upon you for anything, Waley—I know that quite well.'

'So you can,' said the gratified Waley. 'I'll soon find something for him to do. I have taken, somehow, a great fancy for the lad.'

'Yes; he's a very good fellow,' Rose said, with an air of indifference. 'Where are you off to, Waley?'

Waley had not had any intention of going off anywhere just then; but he took the hint and got up.

'Do you want me to come to you at the Voyagers' later on?' Waley asked.

'Voyagers'? No, I think not; I don't think I need trouble you.'

'Coffin is coming, ain't he?'

'Coffin? Oh yes, Coffin is coming, by the way. Yes, ·yes, so he is. But I need not trouble you—just yet, at all events.'

'All right,' said the obedient Waley; and he took his leave. But he was thinking

to himself as he went out of the room.
'Can't make out the chief these last few
days,' he was saying to himself. 'He
promised me I should know everything,
and so far I don't know anything. And
Coffin is to see him to-night, and I am
not to see him. Odd! He says he don't
want to trouble me; but, by Jove! it
troubles me a good deal to be left out of
the swim in all this.'

Suddenly he heard the voice of his chief
calling after him. His mind brightened
as he ran quickly back.

'I am to go to the Voyagers', after all,'
he said to himself.

'Oh, it's only this, Waley. I don't
think I shall be at home all day to-
morrow, and it isn't worth while giving
you the trouble of coming here. Good-
night.'

'What a lot of scruple about giving me
trouble!' Waley said to his own heart.
'Something new, all this awful care about

not giving me trouble!' He lighted another cigar as he stood on the threshold. 'It's awfully early,' he thought. 'I don't quite well know what to do with myself.'

CHAPTER XXII.

WHAT MR. WALEY DID WITH HIMSELF.

WALEY wandered forth into the evening air, his mind filled with all manner of vague, inarticulate thoughts. Something had happened, he could not help thinking —something which was to alter the course of his life. He did not know what it was or what it could be ; but the words which his chief had lately spoken kept ringing in his ears and in his memory.

' Epoch-making days !'

He had not thought of such a thing before. He had not realized any such idea, even when Sir Francis Rose had talked about the epoch-making days ; but now, somehow, he began to find a problem and

a study in it. Is it possible that this was
to be an epoch-making day for him ?
Why had Marmaduke Coffin been summoned to a council from which he was
to all appearance to be deliberately shut
out ?

He suddenly remembered that he had
not yet had any dinner. He was so much
accustomed to dine with the chief when
they both had an evening to spend together,
that he had not realized the fact that he
was to dine alone on an evening when the
chief was to see Marmaduke Coffin later
on at the Voyagers', and when he might
have expected to dine with the chief, or,
at least, to have a later appointment at the
club.

'Come,' he said to himself cheerily; 'I
have not been enjoying myself much
lately. I'll go and have a good dinner
somewhere, and then I'll go and have a
good laugh at one of the halls '—meaning
thereby, of course, one of the music-halls.

So, after a moment of deliberation, he called a hansom, and drove to the Café Royal in Regent Street. ' 'Twill do me a lot of good,' he said to himself, ' and knock the cobwebs off me.'

He found a small table unoccupied at the Café Royal, and he ordered a nice little dinner and some champagne, and determined to start an evening's enjoyment. And as he was waiting for his dinner, his eyes happened to fall upon a mirror in front of him, and in it he saw a weary, deeply-lined, haggard, and almost tragical face ; and after a second or two of wonder as to why anybody apparently in such a dismal mood should ever come into such a place of entertainment, he suddenly realized the fact that the face of the dismal Johnnie was his own countenance. He started a little, and then he said to himself :

' Quite time to go to one of the halls and be made to laugh : something's the matter with me.'

Then, as they were setting his soup
before him, he saw another dismal face
passing by him—a face as dismal as his
own. And he recognised this other
Knight of the Rueful Countenance, and he
hailed him :

'I say, Mr. Conrad, where are you
going to ? come and sit here along o'
me.'

And Jim Conrad stopped, and Conrad's
melancholy phiz broke into a smile as he
saw Waley, and Conrad sat down beside
him with right goodwill, and ordered a
dinner. And the pint of champagne was
countermanded, and a goodly quart bottle
was set upon the table.

'You look as if you were down upon
your luck,' Waley · observed by way of
greeting to his friend.

'I was just going to say the same of
you,' Conrad sympathetically observed,
after he had settled down.

'No; were you really, now? How

very odd! I'm so glad to have caught hold of you.'

'Thanks. I'm very glad to have been caught hold of.'

The sound of Waley's friendly voice was musical in the young man's ears just then.

'I'm rather inclined for a spree to-night,' Waley said. 'Have you anything on hand? I had a sort of notion of going to one of the music-halls. I want to be set laughing. What do you say?'

'All right. I'll go and laugh—if I can.'

The conversation languished. There was a long pause. The two were alone at their table, quite away from the rest of the little world.

'Have a pull at the fizz,' Waley said.

'Thanks,' Conrad answered, and he finished a glass of champagne at a draught.

Still the talk, somehow, did not flow.

'Anything the matter with you, old man?' Waley asked after another interval, as he scanned with kindliness his companion's face.

'I don't know that there is anything very particular, or unexpected, at all events. But what about you?'

'About me? Well, I don't know.'

There was another pause, and the courses of the dinner went and came.

Then Waley suddenly said:

'There was something the chief was saying to me the other day—and it did not quite take hold of me at the time— but now I begin to feel that it bit in: I can't tell you the why and the wherefore, but there it is. It has caught on to me, somehow.'

'Yes; what was it?'

'Well, it was like this, don't you know. The chief asked me, says he, "Don't you find that there are some days which are epoch-making days?" Yes, I am sure those

were his words, Conrad—may I call you
Conrad?'

'Oh yes, by all means; why not?'

'We are friends, ain't we?'

'Yes, I hope so.'

'I feel very friendly to you, anyhow.'

'Well, and so do I to you,' Conrad
said, not without a half-note of impatience
in his voice.

'That's all right. You are a man I
know I can trust, and I tell you that you
can trust me.'

'You needn't tell me. I do trust you.'

'All right. What were we talking
about?'

'About what Rose called epoch-making
days.'

'Yes, yes—how did it pass for a moment
out of my head? Well, he asked me if I
didn't find that some days seemed to be
epoch-making days—when one felt that
something was going to happen that might
change the whole run of one's life.'

' Yes ; and what did you say ?'

' Well, I said—like a fool, I suppose—that I hadn't ever particularly noticed anything of the kind. Have you ever had any such ideas about any day that ever made an impression upon you ?'

' Yes, Waley, I have had such ideas.'

Jim's mind went back at once to the day when he found his mystic ring, and he felt that that was indeed an epoch-making day in his life.

' See that, now ! I suppose it was want of education and book-reading and poetry, and all that sort of thing, in me; but do you know, I never had any thought of the kind in my mind up to that time.'

' Not up to that time ? And now ?'

' Now I think I do begin to understand the feeling. I have a strong notion in my mind that these last few days mean something to me—something that may mean a big change in my life—only I don't know what it is all about, or what is going to come of it. No, not the least little bit in the world.'

'Why trouble yourself about it, Waley?'

'Lord bless you! how do I know? I can't help troubling myself about it. The feeling is there, don't you know. I can't get rid of it.'

Jim began to listen with some genuine interest to his friend's vague outpouring as to his condition of mind. He had come to have a high opinion of Waley's robust and manly good sense, and he well knew that up to that time Waley's one central idea had been that of a spaniel-like devotion to his master. Whatever doubt or brooding was in his mind must, Jim felt assured, be a doubt or brooding on that subject. The doubt or the brooding coincided very curiously with certain doubts which had been springing up in Jim's own mind during the last few days. But he did not want to get any deeper into Waley's confidence than Waley was him-

self willing that he should penetrate. So
he remained silent for a moment or two.
Then Waley began again, as if with an
effort to toss the whole subject away.

‘ Well, well,’ he said, ‘ there’s on use in
making ourselves uncomfortable by talking
over all that kind of gloomy thing now.
You are right about that—why trouble
ourselves ?   When the thing comes, whatever it is, we shall know all about it, eh ?
Look here, let’s talk of something else.
How about Patagonia ?’

‘ About Patagonia?   Yes, what about
Patagonia ?’

‘ When shall you be ready to go out
there ?’

Nothing had been farther from Jim’s
mind for many days than the idea of his
going out to Patagonia just then.

‘ I don’t quite understand what you
want of me in Patagonia.’

‘ Well, if it comes to that, no more do
I.   But the chief is very keen about it.’

' What does he want me to do in Patagonia?'

' Oh, that, of course, he'll tell you.
He always knows exactly what he wants.
I can tell you enough to start you ; when
you are ready to go, he'll tell you all the
rest.'

' Waley,' said Jim gravely, ' I have
something to do in London just now.
When that is over, I am ready to go to
Patagonia or any other part of the world
as soon as you want me to go—the sooner
the better for me.'

' Will it take long?' Waley asked in a
low and kindly tone.

' Will what take long ?'

' Oh, come ! don't you see—the thing
that you want to settle.'

It occurred to Jim that it might take
long indeed if he were to attempt a final
settlement of that trouble—that it might
admit of no final settlement—that the
best efforts he could make might only

tend to unsettlement. But he merely
answered :

' I can't tell you just yet, Waley.'

' The chief wants you to go at once—at
once.'

' Has he told you so ?'

' Told me so to-day.'

And even as Waley was speaking the
thought went across his mind for the first
time : ' Why does the chief want this young
fellow out of London ?'   And then another
flash of guesswork came on him, and he
sat following its light in his uncouth sort
of way, and there was silence again for a
moment or two.

' You're in trouble, old pal, ain't you ?'
he began, in the kindliest tone his voice
could assume ; ' and I wonder if you might
tell me what it is.   I'm ever so much
older than you, and I've knocked about
the world twenty times more than you
have.   Could I help you at all ?'

' No, Waley—thanks, my dear fellow.

I am afraid there is nothing to be done. And I am not sure that the world would call it a trouble of mine. Well, I couldn't explain even if I had any right to explain ; and I am not a very good hand at explanation, anyhow.'

'Nobody is who feels a thing,' Waley said sympathetically. 'Why, I have a doubt and a trouble on my own mind just at this moment, and be hanged if I could explain them to myself, not to talk of explaining them to other folk. But your trouble — don't think me rude or too curious—it is something about a woman, ain't it, now ?'

He put his big hand gently and kindly on Jim Conrad's knee.

Jim winced a little, flushed a little, and then said manfully :

'Yes, Waley, old man, I don't mind confessing to you that much : it is about a woman. Don't ask me any more.'

'My dear boy, not another word. I've

been through that sort of thing myself—
lots of times. You say I can't help you
at all?'

Jim shook his head.

'Could the chief help you?'

The question was put in perfect innocence, but it made Jim Conrad start and
wince and grow red.

'No—no—no!' he said sharply. 'I
don't care to talk about the matter any
more, Waley.'

Now, the vague suspicion that had
come up at first in Waley's mind was an
idea that Conrad might be in love with
some girl, whose attractions had somehow got hold of the chief also. Waley
firmly believed the chief to be irresistible
in his love-making, and Waley's general
notions of women were drawn from experiences in which educated varieties of
taste did not reckon for very much.
Waley had accepted as a position govern-
ing all others the fact that the chief was

irresistible to women. If he was irresistible to one woman, why not to all
women ? Was not that the common-
sense of it ? So he took it at once for
granted that Jim Conrad's trouble was
simply because his ' mash,' as Waley
would have called her, had taken it into
her silly feminine head to fall in love with
Sir Francis Rose. He spoke out on the
spur of the moment—incautious to those
whom he believed to be his friends, while
cautious as a Red Indian to human beings
of the outer range.

' I don't think you need have any
trouble of mind about the chief in that
way, Conrad, my son,' he said, with a
genial, reassuring smile.

' In what way ?' Jim asked, all amazed.

' Oh, well, don't you know, in that
way. Look here, I'll tell you a secret,
and of course you won't breathe a word
of it to a mortal. It's this: the chief
has fallen in love—with whom do you

think ?—you would never guess—with
his own wife! Yes, sure as death! And
I am confoundedly sorry for it, because
it may spoil him for many a good enterprise. Oh, by Jove! these women—how
they do come across us at every hand's
turn! Yes, he's fallen in love with his
own wife all over again, and he wants
to get her back to him, and, I tell you,
if he wants to get her back he'll get her
back! I suppose, anyhow, it's better than
falling in love with some woman who
isn't his wife—more moral and all that.
I say, old man, this ought to be good
news for you, and yet somehow you don't
look quite as if it was. I say, sit up and
tell us what is the matter.'

Jim had indeed, for the moment, fallen
quite out of time. He could hardly catch
on at first to the train of ideas which
Waley had in his mind when Waley endeavoured to reassure him by telling him
that the chief had fallen in love again with

the chief's own wife. Even still it was
but a vague perception of the notion that
came over him. That, however, was a
poor, and altogether secondary, consideration. The one thought uppermost in his
mind was fixed upon Waley's declaration
that Rose had again fallen in love with
his wife, and was determined to get her
back.

‘ I can't believe it, Waley,’ he exclaimed.
‘ He doesn't care three straws about her.
He deserted her; he cast her away ; he
flung her from him in her youth and
her beauty ; and—oh, good heavens! what
am I talking about ?’

‘ Blest if I know,’ Waley said very
gravely, while, for all his disclaimer of
knowledge, a shrewd suspicion was beginning to creep in and to light its little
glow-worm lamp, or firefly lamp, as it
might be, in the dusk of uncertainty.

‘ Oh, that's the way,’ he said to his own
soul.

'Never mind, Waley,' Jim said hurriedly; 'let's not talk of this any more. I don't suppose I quite know what I am talking about. I say, did I drink too much of that champagne?'

'No, 'tain't that,' Waley said in a kindly tone. 'Just look at the bottle, and help yourself again, and then pass it on. Don't you see?'

By this time Waley, with his natural shrewdness, pricked further on by the secrecy of the chief, had come to the conviction that something serious was being planned about which he had not been consulted, and was not to be consulted, and which threatened to be serious for Jim Conrad. The rights and the wrongs of the matter were wholly unknown to him; but he was very anxious to know something about them. Suddenly he started off on the track of blunt inquiry, and, having gulped down another glass of champagne, he burst out :

'I say, look here, old pal : you haven't been making love to the chief's wife, or anything of that kind, have you ?'

Poor Jim's barrier of reserve quite broke down.

'I didn't know she was his wife,' he said—the conversation was carried on almost in a whisper—'I didn't know she was anybody's wife.'

'Oh, but you do know now ?'

'Oh yes, I do know now ; she told me.'

'What do you mean to do ?'

'To save her from him, if I can. He's a brute and a beast and a scoundrel !'

'Look here, Conrad,' Waley interposed not ungently ; 'I can't stand hearing this said of the chief ; it wouldn't be proper on my part, and I shan't.'

'All right,' Conrad replied ; 'then you need not stand it. I shall leave you to yourself. Good-night.'

So Conrad started up from the table.

'Now, now, now!' Waley said soothingly. 'See how hot and hasty you young
chaps are. Sit down again, Conrad, my
son. By Jove! you might be a son of
mine, so far as years go, anyhow. Look
here: I am a good deal on your side of this
business lately, although I know very little
about it.'

'I can't tell you anything,' said Jim,
sitting down again, however.

'Don't want you to tell me a word more
than you feel at liberty to tell to a true
friend, if my honourable friend will allow
me so to call him,' Waley said, with a vague
recollection of what he had heard now and
then, when he sat in one of the galleries of
the House of Commons.

'Well, there,' Jim murmured: 'I was in
love with her before I knew that she was
married, and she had no reason to tell me
her secret at first; but when she found out
that I was in love with her—when I told
her so, in fact—then she let me know that

she was married, and that her husband had
deserted her, and that there could be
nothing between us—between her and me
—but only friendship, and that at a dis-
tance. Oh, good God! how I felt! I
knew that her husband was a scoundrel,
but I didn't know who he was.'

'Now, now! You only know one side
of the story.'

'See here, Waley. Has he deserted his
wife, or has he not?'

'Well, if you press me for an answer, I
am afraid he has.'

'And, now, does he want to get her
back ?'

'Oh yes; I told you so. He has fallen
madly in love with her all over again.'

'Yes. But does he know that she has
lately come in for a large fortune—does he
know that, Waley?'

'I am afraid he does know that—in fact,
he told me so.'

'And is that the renewal of love ?'

'Well, you see, the chief is a man of what people call a complex character. I suppose the money may have something to do with it.'

'Yes; I dare say,' Jim interjected grimly.

'I know—I know; but I don't think it has everything to do with it. I don't believe it's the money and nothing else. The chief is a sort of man who can't bear to be cut out of anything or left out of anything. So long as he had merely dropped the young woman, it didn't seem to matter much to him. Stay, now; I'm only putting the case from his point of view, and it's no use fussing. But, of course, when it came to his wanting to get hold of the young woman again, and she not wanting to be got hold of by him, why, that, don't you see, is another pair of shoes. Well, now, what do you propose to do ? He is her husband, ain't he ?'

'Unhappily, he is.'

' He hasn't lost any of his rights—he hasn't deserted for long enough, has he?'

' Unhappily, no.'

' Very well. Then, where do you come in? You don't want her to run away with you, now, do you?'

' Waley, don't talk in that infernal way. I wonder what she would say to me if I were to hint at such a thing.'

'I know—I know,' Waley said in a conciliatory tone, not meaning that he knew precisely what words the lady would use under such conditions, but that he knew she would say exactly what Jim Conrad assumed that she would be sure to say.

' She isn't like the women we meet in the world, Waley. I want you from the first—from the very first—to understand that.'

' Yes, yes, of course—I quite understand that. The chief told me as much as that himself. He took it all upon himself—said it was all his own fault, and that he was not worthy of her—you know that sort of thing,' Waley added with the best purpose, but with, perhaps, a little want of tact.

'She is the purest and the noblest woman that ever lived!' Jim burst out again, and then shot an eager glance around him to make sure that nobody had heard him.

'Yes, yes; of course she is—they all are,' Waley said again with the kindest purpose, but again with a little want of tact. 'But, you see, that only makes the difficulty all the greater. What do you propose to do? You know that she is married; you know that her husband is going to claim her again; you know that she is a woman who wouldn't run away with you or anyone else. Then, what in the world do you propose to do?'

'I'll tell you what I propose to do, Waley. I am not such a fool as you sup-pose——'

'Never said you were a fool of any sort, dear boy—never supposed it. Give you my word of honour.'

'Doesn't matter—doesn't matter whether you did or not. What I want to do now is to get her free from him—if I can. If I feel sure that she is free from him, I shall be content never to see her again. Yes, I shall! I should be willing to enter into a bond never to see her again, never, never, in all my life, if only I could know that she was free from him. And to bring that about, Waley, I'll do all that I can, and I tell you I shall think little of any possible danger to myself if I can secure that freedom for her.'

'You are a good chap,' Waley said slowly, 'and I believe in my soul you mean all that you say. But how do you propose to get her away from him?'

'She has friends,' Jim answered. 'She has one great friend—a woman—who will go to the farthest end of the earth with her. I shall help them to get away.'

'You can't. He will find them out. He will do anything when he has set his heart upon it.'

'His heart! His heart! Has he any heart?'

'Well, I thought he had once upon a time, and I hope he has still. I do believe, honest Injin, that he has set his heart upon her again. I do believe that he is really in love with her. He's an awfully odd sort of man, but he'll have his way.'

'Waley,' said Conrad, speaking in a low, suppressed tone, 'sooner than that he should get hold of her again I'll kill him.'

'My good fellow,' Waley answered, in the calmest voice, 'if you come between him and any design of his he is much more likely to kill you.'

Waley meant what he said. During all their talk he had been turning over in his mind some vague possibilities.

' Let him, if he can,' Conrad said. ' I'll
see to that! If I am attacked from behind
I can't protect myself, and my life, like the
life of everybody else, is at the mercy of
any assassin. Why, there was a man killed
not fifty yards from this very place last
night, here in the West End of London!
I can only take my chance of that. If
anyone attacks me from the front, I fancy
I can give a good account of myself and
of him. But I'll not let him get hold of
her if I can help it. No, not if I were to
kill him!'

' Let us think this over,' Waley said,
' and talk it over another time, as soon as
we can. I want to pass it all through my
mind, do you see, and size it up, if I can,
and see what it all comes to. We are
talking of killing as if we were in some
parts of the world where I have been, and
where anybody who likes kills anybody he
dislikes, and very few questions asked
about the business afterwards. But I'll

look into the matter, and tell you what
idea I get of it. It wants some cool
thinking over. Of course, we keep all
this to ourselves for the present?'

' Of course—of course.'

' Very good. I'll let you know. I
dare say you don't feel much inclined for
any of the halls to-night?'

' Oh no ; not I.'

' No more do I. Let's go.'

So they parted. Waley kept asking
himself, as he wandered towards his
lodgings :

' Was it for this Coffin was brought
over? Or for this and something else?'

He had had Sir Francis Rose's own
assurance that he meant to get hold of his
wife by fair means or foul, and that idea at
the time did not seem wholly to shock
Waley's moral sense, which, indeed, had
stood a good deal of shocking already.
But it was clear that, since he had failed
quite to fall in enthusiastically with his

patron's ideas on this subject, he had been left somewhat out in the shade, and this very night he had noticed how the face of the chief grew dark when he spoke of the necessity of getting Conrad out of the way —to.Patagonia, or anywhere else.

And now Coffin was on the scene, and Coffin had been summoned over in the first instance, and according to the usual fashion, through him, Waley; and now, behold, he was put aside, and Coffin was taken into lonely confidence. Was it that Coffin was summoned in the first instance to help in nothing but the carrying off of Rose's own wife—an enterprise in which Waley might possibly have been expected to assist? Was it possible that now his help might be required for a darker deed? Waley's much revolving mind brooded deeply over this possibility as he went his way through the flashing and clattering streets.

CHAPTER XXIII.

WHAT THE CHIEF DID WITH HIMSELF.

WHILE all this conference was going on between Jim Conrad and Mr. Waley at the Café Royal, Sir Francis Rose was dining alone at the Voyagers' Club. He talked to nobody when he could avoid it ; and the Voyagers' Club was rather a social, conversational, friendly, chatty little club —not at all like the monumental old-fashioned clubs of the Waterloo Place region, or the overcrowded and noisy 'caravanserais' of the Northumberland Avenue quarter. It was not, however, the humour of Sir Francis Rose to talk this night, and to those who approached him he soon made it clear that good-fellowship was not the sort of thing he wanted then. He had a way of conveying his sentiments very clearly without drawing on any great store of eloquence, and the few who accosted him on this particular evening promptly recognised the fact that he wanted to be let alone. At the Voyagers' Club people did not mind that.

Almost everybody had now and then on his mind a new expedition or enterprise of some kind which had to be carefully thought out, and which would not be the better for even the friendliest interruption. So there was no fault found with Rose, and he was allowed to think undisturbed over his enterprise—whatever it might be.

Rose had just now a good deal to think over. There was new matter in his mind, and his mental balance was a little shaken by the novelty of emotion which he had allowed to take possession of him.

Love had since his very boyhood been a

familiar, a welcome, a delightful disturber
of his heart.   But how about hate?   Hate
had not up to this counted for much in the
self-centred nature of Francis Rose.   He
had, of course, in his varied career had
many an outburst of sudden angry passion,
taking to itself for the hour the mood of
hate.   He had killed a man more than
once in his time—and in countries where,
as Waley said to Conrad, if you do kill a
man, nobody takes much trouble about a
prosecution at criminal law.

But the intense pleasure that Rose had
always found in new sensation had generally
been the excitement of risk and of danger;
of success or failure in enterprise; the
excitement of love-making; the excitement of studying himself under new
conditions.   Now, however, he found the
keen sensation of intense hatred taking
fast grip on him.   He felt himself hating
Jim Conrad, and according to his fashion
he cherished the new feeling, and cuddled

it, and made much of it, and was determined to give it its head.

Just at the moment when he had become
inflamed again with love for the wife
whom he had not merely abandoned, but
thrust from him with his cruel parting
message conveyed through the ring and its
inscription—just as he had resolved to win
back her love, to conquer her and to
capture her—just as he had found that to
get her back would be to become possessed
of money enough to enable him to take
again that place in society which he had
wantonly thrown away and now was
passionately eager to recover—just at that
crisis came in the young man who stood,
as Rose was convinced, in the way of his
reconquering his wife's affections.   He
had no doubt that Jim Conrad was madly
in love with Clelia Rose; and how if
Clelia Rose were in love with Jim Conrad?
It was quite possible.   He, Francis Rose,
had cast her off; he had sent her that ring,

with its confounded message telling her
bluntly that their love-story had all come
to an end.

What in the world had possessed him,
he now asked himself, to do such a thing?
Why could he not have remained away as
other adventurous husbands do, until it
suited him to come back—and never come
back if he did not feel inclined for a move
that way? But he must be theatric; he
must be romantic; he must have a new
sensation; he must do things in a way that
no one had done things before. He well
remembered the impulse that came on
him. The ring was a copy of an old
family ring which had come down to
Clelia's father, who had the duplicate
wrought in India, and gave it to Clelia,
and Clelia had given it to Rose in Paris
just before their marriage, and asked him
to wear it day and night for her sake.
Then they had invented, together, their
fantastic little anagram—Rosita to Francisco

—and had it enamelled on the ring. And
then—and then—and then he had made
some excuse, after the first year of their
marriage, for leaving her and wandering
off on one of his enterprises. He pro-
pitiated himself by remembering that it
was only after she had found him out, and
had reproached him, and had told him that
he was not the man she believed herself to
have married, he first wanted to get away
and be free ; and the idea at last occurred
to him to get the ring engraved inside with
signs that might signify the close of their
married life, and so send it to her to let her
know that all was over between her and
him. He well remembered—and he felt
a self-comforting pride in the recollection
—that at the time he really thought he
was conveying his announcement of the
inevitable in a very considerate, graceful,
and romantic form, such as might possibly
even soothe the morbid feelings of a young
married woman whose husband did not

find himself able to put up with married
life any longer. Even still he could not
help thinking that the thing, as it had to be
done—and he was convinced then that it
had to be done—was put into generous,
regretful, and even tender shape.

But, oh! how he wished now that it
never had been done! Why, even if he
had been absent for many more years than
he actually was absent, he could have
invented any tale of a wrecked ship, a
desert island, a capture by savages—anything, anything ! Clelia had so trusting
a nature that, if he had only managed her
well, he was sure he could have got her
to believe that he had been captured by a
Barbary rover, and sold into slavery among
the Paynims. Now he saw clearly what
he might have so easily done and said :

'I hated myself, Clelia—I had forfeited
your love—I had forfeited it deservedly—
I could not endure civilization any more,
or the sight of the place in which we had

once been happy, and so I rushed off to the
wildest regions I could find, longing for
death, striving for death, and with only one
hope in my heart, that when she heard of
my early fate Clelia would feel sorry for
me, and forgive me !'

Why, to be sure, that would have been
the right thing to do ! That would have
fetched her—that would have fetched any
nice woman. But he had spoiled all with
his absurd valedictory ceremony and her
confounded old ring. And now in came
this young fellow with his youth and his
sentiment—and a horribly well - set - up
young fellow too—and he went and fell in
love with Clelia, and who on earth was to
say that she had not fallen in love with
him ? Some men would throw her over
for ever, acknowledging all the while that
it was their own infernal bungling that had
made the mess.

'But I am not the man to do that sort
of thing,' Sir Francis said to his own soul,

with proud self-appreciation. 'She did love me once, and she shall love me again. I'll make her; by Jove! I'll tame her. I'll carry her off if I have to keep her in a cage. A week of imprisonment will bring her round to me. And as for him!'

Oh, if they were only in some of the far-off regions which he had studied not wisely but too well! Something must be done with him. If Waley could not manage to send him out to Patagonia or some such place — and Waley seemed, somehow, like chilling off this last day or two—why, then, it must be seen what counsel with Marmaduke Coffin had to offer. A good fellow, Marmaduke Coffin —a thorough good fellow, afraid of nothing, sticking at nothing. Yes, it must be seen what Marmaduke Coffin would have to advise.

And at that moment a waiter came and told him that a gentleman wished to see him—Mr. Marmaduke Coffin.

Sir Francis Rose almost started as he heard the name. He knew, of course, that Coffin was coming; he was expecting him, he had ordered him to come, he had fixed this place and the hour, and yet he almost started when at that precise moment he heard the announcement of Coffin's name. It was as if in some old story a sudden purpose of evil had called up in bodily presence some demon agent to press it on and carry it out.

Sir Francis Rose was not easily startled, and the shudder soon passed off, and he felt ashamed of himself for having felt even the slight and momentary shock. After all, no mortal can be always a perfect master of himself. The saint has his moments of shrinking from martyrdom. The bravo sometimes starts at a shadow, and fears each bush an officer.

Rose gave directions that Coffin should be shown into the little recess with which we are already well acquainted, in front of the window in one of the corridors, where people sometimes smoked who did not care to mount up to the regular smoking-room. It was Rose's fixed and deliberate belief that conspiracy of any kind was most safely carried on in public. A recess in a corridor just near a flight of stairs, with people always going up and down—who could suspect anything of conspiracy there?

Rose found Marmaduke Coffin in this little recess. Coffin rose and bowed as if he were greeting a conspirator of a higher class than himself—nothing more. Then Rose ordered cigars and whisky and soda. That being accomplished, and the waiter having disappeared, Rose came to business at once.

'I am glad you have come, Coffin.'

'Of course I came,' Coffin answered.

'Yes. You are not a man of many scruples, Coffin. I have always known that of you.'

' Haven't any scruples,' Coffin replied.

' Of course not ; no sensible man has.'

' Waley has,' Coffin said.

Sir Francis started once again, and looked into Coffin's impassive face, trying to find an expression of meaning there. He found none. Coffin seemed like a man who is propounding some abstract scientific truth.

' Yes, Waley has scruples ; I have found that out,' Rose said after a moment's pause, during which he had been questioning himself as to whether Coffin could possibly have divined what was passing in the mind of his chief. Rose might as well have sought an explanation of what the blotting-pad was thinking by staring on the blotting-pad's ink-besmirched surface.

' You have your own ambition, Coffin.'

' I have my own ambition.'

' Yes, I know. Come now, what is it ? You have not got much out of our joint enterprises so far, have you ?'

' Nothing at all.'

' Of course, I know that. But you still expect ?'

' I still expect.'

' What do you want ?'

' I want to be my own master.'

' Come, I quite understand that sort of ambition. Now then, what sort of mastership do you want to have ?'

' I should like to set up a hair-cutting and hairdressing shop of my own—Rue de la Paix, Paris.'

Rose would have liked to smile, but knew that any such expression of amusement would be ill-timed. He was, however, intensely amused. Fancy what human ambition can come to! A man of no scruples, who would do anything for the privilege of being the boss of a hairdresser's shop in the Rue de la Paix! After all, was it not, in the sense of true philosophy, as good an ambition as that of any other man ? In the eyes of a Superior Power, what is the essential difference between the man whose ambition it is to reign over a hairdresser's shop, and the man whose ambition it is to reign over a cabinet or over a kingdom?

The thought passed through Rose's mind like a flash, and he did not allow a moment's silence to give Coffin the idea that there was anything odd about his idea of a goal in life.

'I know the shop I should like to have,' Coffin added, in an unwonted burst of effusiveness.

'The place where you have been working yourself?' Rose asked, with a sudden inspiration.

'That place. It is to be bought. It isn't doing very well of late. I could buy it if I had the money, and I could make it pay. Five thousand pounds. Not francs—pounds.'

'The money is yours,' Rose said

promptly, 'if you can manage to do what I want to have done.'

'Tell me.'

'I'll tell you in a moment or two. But first I am anxious to know a little more about this ambition of yours. Is there nothing behind it but the bossing of the shop?'

This time Coffin's features relaxed into something that might almost be called a smile.

'You are very clever, chief,' he said. 'There is something more.'

'Tell me what it is.'

'Well, I know a nice little girl who I think would marry me if I got to be the owner of that shop.'

Rose smiled quite undisguisedly.

'A Paris girl?' he asked.

'A Paris girl, yes.'

'But, my good Coffin, you have a wife of your own, here in London.'

'They wouldn't know anything about

that in Paris,' Coffin replied with perfect composure.

' And you are prepared to run the risk ?'

' Wouldn't be any risk.'

' Does she know that you have a wife ?'

' No ; I don't mean to tell her.'

Rose was quite delighted with this new proof of Coffin's freedom from the slavery of conventional scruple.

' This is the man for me,' he thought.

' What do you want done ?' Coffin asked, as calmly as if he were asking a customer whether he wanted shampooing as well as hair-cutting.

Rose was once more delighted.

' Well, look here ; I want a man got out of the way somewhere.'

' All right ; tell me his name.'

Rose drew back a little from this absolute and unconditional readiness; he hastened to qualify:

' Understand, Coffin, I don't want any violence.'

' Of course not,' Coffin answered tranquilly ; ' no one ever does.'

And something faintly resembling a smile again crossed his solemn countenance.

' I see you understand things,' Rose said.

' Yes, I understand things.'

' And you quite understand that I don't want any violence ?'

' I quite understand, if it can possibly be avoided.'

' Yes, yes, if it can possibly be avoided, of course,' his chief hurriedly said. ' Only you know that I am not counselling any act of violence—you quite understand that? What ?'

' I quite understand that you are not counselling any act of violence, only you want the man out of the way.'

' Yes, if he can't be prevailed upon to

take himself out of the way and let me be
rid of him.'

' Prevailed upon by you, or by me ?'

' Prevailed upon by Waley.'

' I see.   Waley tries to talk him over,
and if Waley fails, then I come in ?'

' That's about it.'

' That's about it,' Coffin echoed con-
templatively.

' You've got the whole business.'

' And no questions asked ?'

' You may be sure I shan't ask any
questions.   Other people may, of course.'

' They may ; I don't mind about that.'

' But you will remember that I have
not advised you to do anything rash or
violent ?'

' Chief,' said Coffin solemnly, ' a bargain
is a bargain as between man and man.
That's what I always say, and what I say I
stick to.   You give me the money to buy
the house in the Rue de la Paix, and that's
all you have got to do with the business—

except to tell me when Waley has failed in his job, and when I come in.'

'You shall know that in good time. This money—must it be paid all at once, Coffin ?'

'No; I can arrange about that. If I have your word, I can manage the business myself at any time that suits you.'

'You have my word, Coffin; you can trust me.'

'I trust you,' Coffin said grimly. 'And now, will you tell me the man's name, and whereabouts he is likely to be found ?'

'You know the man already.'

'Do I ? That makes it all the easier to manage. What is he called ?'

Then Rose bent over and whispered a name.

No gleam of surprise or emotion of any kind passed over Coffin's face.

'Thought he was going out to Patagonia,' he said, after a moment of silence, and with gloomy, unabated coolness.

'I wanted him to go, but he seems to be backing out of it. He appears to prefer London just now,' Rose added, with a bitterness of tone which he could not repress, which it relieved him not to repress, although in another instant he told himself that he was a fool for expressing any emotions during the arrangement of such a purely business transaction.

'Don't wonder,' Coffin said; 'I shouldn't like to have to go out to Patagonia just now.'

'No,' Sir Francis said, with a half-smile. 'The Rue de la Paix has more charms—and the wife Number Two!'

'Right you are,' Coffin responded, without even half a smile.

'But don't you know that wife Number Two is a dangerous business? You may be extradited and brought over here and tried for bigamy.'

Somehow or other, although Coffin was Rose's chosen instrument, and seemed made for the purpose, there was something about his imperturbable coolness that irritated Rose.   With all his physical daring, Rose felt that there were things he could not take so coolly, and it annoyed him.

'Nothing venture, nothing have,' said Coffin, in tone as earnest as if the proverb were then spoken for the first time on earth.   'I run that risk for the woman—I run the other risk for the house.'

'The other risk?'

'The risk of the removal, don't you know!'

Was Coffin really trying to make a joke? The answer never can be given.

'The removal!   What removal?'

'The removal of our friend, who don't want to visit Patagonia.   Don't wonder at him.   Patagonia must be a very stupid place.'

'To anyone who has lived in the Rue de la Paix.'

'That's it.'

'Come in to-morrow. Waley is not coming.'

'All right.'

'Well, I suppose we have said enough.'

Rose stood up. He put it not peremptorily, but gently. He was anxious to conciliate as far as he possibly could. But he began to find something uncanny, even to him, in the indifference of his follower to all risks and to all codes.

'Said all we want to, Sir Francis? Too much talk never of any use between men who understand each other.'

'Won't you have another whisky and soda?'

'No, thanks. Don't care much for drinks.'

'Another cigar, then?'

'Well, yes—another cigar—just to carry me home.'

He had his cigar, and he went his way. As he crossed St. James's Square he murmured to himself:

'Thought I should get hold of that house in the end.   Knew I should.   Hope that young fellow won't take it into his silly head to knock under, and go to Patagonia after all.'

CHAPTER XXIV.

'WHAT IS TO BE DONE FIRST?'

'What is to be done—above all, what is to be done first?' Such was the thought that was rushing round and round in Jim Conrad's bewildered mind, like the blind wave in the cavern, the long sea-hall, which Tennyson pictured. Such was the thought that surged and stormed blindly enough, and beat for a while all purpose-lessly in poor Conrad's mind as he left Mr. Waley's company on that epoch-making night. It was now clear that Rose had determined to get back his deserted wife by force, if needs were; and in such force he would unquestionably, as Waley had pointed out, have at least the traditions of English law on his side. Jim did not care three straws about the threatened danger to himself. He would not have minded, anyhow; it would not have turned him from his purpose for one moment; in such a matter he did not hold his life at a pin's fee. But, in fact, he did not now believe there was any such danger. He reasoned, as most of us do, from our common daily experience.

' I have never heard of assassinations after the Sicilian or the Corsican fashion in England,' he would have said ; ' and I don't believe that anything of the kind is going to be attempted for my especial benefit.'

That danger, therefore, did not really enter into his calculation. But the other was a danger, clear, probable — all but certain. The very sensation of capturing and carrying off in London the wife whom he had deserted would, as Jim knew, be

a delightful experience to a man like
Sir Francis Rose.

But what was to be done? What was
to be done first? It was now ten o'clock—
no more. Could he call at Clelia's hotel
at such an hour, and put her on her
guard? It would be better, much better,
he thought, if in the first instance he were
to see Gertrude Morefield. He could
speak more freely to her; he could learn
from her what were likely to be Clelia's
resolves at such a moment of danger. It
seemed a strange sort of proceeding to call
on a young lady at a West-End hotel
about ten o'clock in the evening; but he
knew that Miss Morefield was not the
least in the world conventional, and that
she would have insisted on the right of
girls to carry latch-keys if she had thought
about such a matter at all. Anything, Jim
told himself, would be better than allowing a whole night to pass without giving
Clelia, directly or indirectly, some warning

of the danger. So he drove to the hotel where the girls were staying, almost as nervous about asking to see a young woman after ten o'clock as if he were doing some deed calculated to fright the isle from its propriety.

Arrived at the hotel, he went to the office, asked to see Miss Morefield, and wrote upon the card he was sending up : ' Important—want to see you particularly,' and deeply underlined the ' you.' He was promptly shown into a small drawing-room, which was quite empty, and the lights of which were turned down. The lights were turned up again, and he was left alone for an anxious moment.

Then he heard a rustle of skirts, and Miss Morefield came into the room. She was looking pale, but very pretty, and was no more discomposed than if it had been Jim's regular habit to call at ten o'clock every night. She quietly shook hands with him, and came to the point at once.

'What is the matter ?' she asked.

'That brings me here so late ?'

She seemed to chafe at the awkward unnecessary question, born of Jim's confusion.

'Yes, yes, tell me. You wanted to see me particularly ?'

'Yes, I wanted to see you, and not Miss Vine—not at first, anyhow.'

'It concerns her, then ?'

'It concerns her.'

'Tell me.'

'Do people come in here much ?' he asked, glancing round at the empty room.

'Not at this hour ; later, yes, when the theatres are over. We can talk here quite safely. Go on.'

'Miss Vine's husband — I mean, of course, Lady Rose's husband—is in London now.'

'I know ; she told me. She has seen him.'

'He is determined that she shall return to him.'

'She will not; she has told me. We have talked it all over. She will die first; she has told me so.'

'All the same, he is determined to get her back.'

'He can't get her back.'

'He will try. You do not know the man. I know a good deal of him, and I know that he is capable of anything.'

'There are laws,' the girl said contemptuously.

'There are no laws that can prevent a husband from resuming his hold over his wife.'

'True!' Gertrude said, with a light of anger flashing triumphantly into her eyes. 'You have said it; there are no laws in this country, or in any other, I suppose, to protect women against the brutal tyranny of men.'

'Well, well,' Conrad said, a little im-

patiently, for he thought the general question of woman's rights and woman's wrongs
was rather out of place just then, and he
did not know how soon some of the theatres
might be closing; 'at all events, I don't
believe there are any laws which would
enable Lady Rose to escape from the con-
trol of her husband.'

He hated speaking of ' Lady Rose,' but
what could he do ?   He could not go on
talking of ' Miss Vine ' escaping from her
husband, and he did not like to speak of
' Clelia.'

Miss Morefield saw this, and frowned a
little.

' Let us call her Clelia,' she said ; ' I
detest to hear her called Lady Rose.'

There was a generous flush on the girl's
face.

' So do I,' said Jim earnestly.

And somehow Gertrude seemed to flush
again.

' Well, what I came for,' Conrad went

on, 'is to warn her of the danger—to warn you in the first instance, for you understand her, and you can tell her all you think she ought to know—and then, if she likes to see me, she can send for me.'

'But you have told me nothing, except that there is danger. Danger of what? There is no danger in his trying to get her to go back to him; she will not go.'

'Then he will carry her off by force!'

'My dear Mr. Conrad, this is not Circassia. This is safe and commonplace London. People don't do these things.'

'I tell you, Miss Morefield, that you are mistaken. This man will do that, or any other thing that he makes up his mind to. I have come at a knowledge which appears to me absolutely certain that he is determined to have her back again, and it will be only a delightful new sensation to him to carry her off by mere force.'

Jim felt somewhat disappointed in Miss Morefield's manner. She did not seem, he thought, as much alarmed as she ought to be about her friend. Poor Jim had his mind full only of one subject, and he made that quite plain. Perhaps he made it just a little too plain under the circumstances. Decidedly, he was not very clever in understanding the feelings of girls.

A change came over Gertrude's manner. She dropped her eyes, and remained silent for a moment. Then she spoke in a much softer tone.

'Mr. Conrad, both she and I have absolute confidence in you, and in your judgment, and in your friendship. If you tell us that you really think there is danger——'

'I know there is,' he exclaimed—'utter danger!'

'Then, I am sure there is danger.'

'I can't tell you how I came to know it,' he said, 'but there it is.'

'We can take it on your word,' she answered with a sweet, resigned kind of smile, which touched Jim Conrad much, although he did not at the moment think of its significance ; 'and it is for you and me to guard her against it. We are her friends.'

' She has no better friends,' Jim declared earnestly.

' She has no other friends now. Well, what can we do ?'

' Had we not better tell her at once ? I mean, had you not better tell her ?'

' Perhaps so—oh yes, I think so. But just a moment first. When do you think this attempt might be made ?'

' I don't know. Any time. This night, perhaps.'

' In this hotel—full of people ?'

' It's not likely, but it would be quite possible. The man is equal to anything. Suppose he gave his name ; suppose he is known here to be the man he represents himself to be ; suppose he claimed his wife ! She couldn't say that she wasn't his

wife; you couldn't say it. Who would
prevent him from taking her in his arms
and carrying her off?'

'This is terrible!' said the girl, turning
pale.

'If I were here,' said Jim, 'I'd kill him
rather than let him carry her off.'

'If I were she,' said Miss Morefield,
'I'd kill myself rather than let him carry
me off, and I hope she'll do it.'

Jim shook his head sadly. The same
thought had sometimes flashed through
his own mind and through his own
heart.

'It mustn't come to that,' he said in a
despondent tone that half belied the assurance of his words.

'If I were she, I'd rather do it,' said the
impetuous little maid, 'than drag out life
in enforced companionship with a wretch
like him.'

'Well, hadn't we better see her and
talk with her?' Jim asked, feeling it

hopeless then and there to argue back to first principles in morals. 'Or would you rather tell it all to her yourself, and send for me to-morrow, supposing that you want me ?'

'Oh no ; you must come now and see her at once. You must tell us what we are to do.'

'All right ; let us go.'

Gertrude led the way. They went upstairs without exchanging a word as they went. Then they reached the sitting-room, and Gertrude opened the door and went in, and said :

'Clelia dear, here is Mr. Conrad.'

Clelia had been leaning on the chimney-piece with head drooping. Before she had time to turn round, Jim had caught sight of the attitude and interpreted it.

The attitude was not that of anxiety, into which doubt and possibility may enter. It was the attitude of one who expects to hear the worst, and only waits in enforced patience until the worst be formally announced.

Then Clelia turned round and gave Jim her hand. It was a hand of marble coldness.

'I knew it was about me when you sent for Gertrude. I knew that you two were conspiring together to save me from some danger—you two—my best, my only friends.'

Jim's heart was touched beyond all expression when he remembered that but a few minutes before Gertrude herself had said just the same thing, in only slightly different words—that she and he were Clelia's only friends.

'You could not have two friends on this earth,' he exclaimed, 'who would go farther to keep you from harm.'

'As if I did not know that!' and with an almost childish impulse of confidence she took for a moment a hand of each in hers, and Jim felt in his very soul that it

would be a rapture for him to die defend-
ing her. 'Well,' Clelia went on, having
put down her outbreak of emotion, 'tell
me your news. I shall not be frightened.
Perhaps I can already guess it.'

'Perhaps you can,' Jim answered sadly ;
and then, as Gertrude seemed to leave him
to tell the tale, he told her in a low, rapid,
but clear voice, just what he had told Miss
Morefield.

'I was afraid it would come to this,'
Clelia said quietly. 'Well, what is to be
done? I will not go back to him. I feel
like some heroine of a melodrama ;' and
she smiled a wan smile. 'I will never be
taken alive.'

'Quite right!' Gertrude exclaimed,
stamping her little foot, and with a
warlike flash from her bright eyes.

'Well, it must not come to that,' Jim
said soothingly.

'But what's the good of saying that?'
Gertrude demanded impatiently, imperi-

ously. 'Tell her what she is to do—how she is to escape.'

In all this confusion, Jim looked with some surprise at the pretty impulsive girl, with the puckered eyebrows and the angry eyes. There were moods of Gertrude to-night which he could not quite understand.

'You must both get away out of this,' he said, as quietly as he could.

'Yes, yes; we know all that. We are not going to stay here to be taken like rats in a hole. Where can Clelia get to this night—this very night? Tell us—tell us. Can't we get to the Continent this very night?'

'You can't go to the Continent to-night,' Jim said. 'There is no train to Dover or Folkestone before the morning.'

'But we can go somewhere—somewhere out of this, can't we?' the unsatisfied girl insisted. 'I don't care where we go, if we only get out of London.'

'Have you much luggage?' asked Jim, thrown into a practical mood of consideration by the girl's impracticable impatience.

'Luggage! luggage! As if we were likely to drag around great piles of Saratoga trunks; or as if it would matter whether we left them behind!'

Now, it was becoming clear to Jim in his practical mood that for the two women to decamp from a West End hotel at eleven o'clock at night would be simply to give Sir Francis Rose or anybody else the easiest way of getting on their track. But he was at first almost afraid to say this, lest Gertrude might think him too easy-going about Clelia's safety—which, indeed, was the last thought likely to come into Gertrude's mind.

'Let us risk this night,' Clelia said, with a quiet smile. 'Night brings counsel, are we not told? and morning brings comfort. To-morrow we may be able to see our

way a little clearer—whether the comfort
comes or not.'

'But suppose something does happen
to-night?' Jim broke in, with a renewal
of his former alarm. 'Suppose he chooses
to make a melodramatic business of it this
very night? I tell you that the man only
lives on sensation, and that his whole life
is one long indulgence in the delight of
new emotions. It might just suit him to
make a grand melodramatic scene here this
very night——'

'But against that we can have no
security,' Clelia said. In her heart she
could not help wondering how entirely
Jim's analysis of her husband's nature and
temperament agreed with her own. 'We
can't get away to-night without giving an
alarm, and calling attention to our flight.
To-morrow we may be able to do something better. Let us part for the night,
Mr. Conrad; and you can come and see
Gertrude and me to-morrow.'

'Yes, I think you are right,' Jim answered, almost reluctantly. 'I don't see that anything much can be done to-night. Anyhow, I am strongly against your going to the Continent. Nobody can cross the Channel in these days without its being found out by anybody who cares to know, and who can follow in a few hours. Much better go to New York. To-morrow— well, I shall have thought something out. I am sure you had better keep in London and lie low for a day or two, but not here, of course—not here. You can't go into a suburb; the people in a suburb always take notice of new-comers. No, no, some crowded central place where strangers are going and coming all day long. How long may I stay here and talk to you?' He looked first at Clelia and then at Gertrude. 'Which of you is hostess?'

'I suppose I ought to be hostess,' Clelia said with composure, 'because I am a married woman. But then, you see, I

don't pass for a married woman here.
Which of us is hostess, Gertrude dear?'

'Oh, how do I know, and what does
it matter? Who cares which of us is
hostess?'

'Well, which of you will tell me how
late I may stay with you to-night? Must
I go before the theatres empty out and
people come back here?'

'If you ask me,' Gertrude said, 'I don't
care three straws.'

'I think,' Clelia interposed, 'you had
better go now, Mr. Conrad. There is
nothing to be gained by seeming to be
eccentric. We are in a country of conventionality.'

'Oh, conventionality!' Gertrude exclaimed, and it seemed as if she could say
no more.

That one word appeared to express
thoughts too deep for words—at all events,
for words that had to be spoken within a
limited lapse of time.

'Come to-morrow, Mr. Conrad,' Clelia said. 'Come to breakfast or to luncheon.'

She spoke with as much quietude as if she were an ordinary London hostess inviting some friend to an every-day sort of entertainment. Jim was immensely impresssed by her courage and her coolness.

'Never mind about breakfast or luncheon,' he said; 'may I come at ten? I shall have thought things out by then, and I don't suppose now that anything will happen to-night. Anyhow, we must chance it.'

'Come at ten by all means,' Clelia answered. 'Nothing will happen to-night.'

Jim was about to take his leave.

'I want to say a word or two to you before I go,' Clelia said. 'Gertrude darling, would you mind leaving us for a few minutes?'

'No,' Gertrude returned, 'not the least

in the world. But I, too, want to say a word to Mr. Conrad before he goes.'

'Oh, do you?' Clelia asked, with a glance of bright good humour.

'Yes, I do,' Gertrude affirmed doggedly. 'So, Clelia, when you have talked with Mr. Conrad, you can go away for the night, don't you see?—I mean, from this room, of course. I shall come to you in your bedroom.'

'Very well, dear,' Clelia answered, and Gertrude disappeared.

The moment she had gone the whole manner of Clelia changed. An intense earnestness settled on her which made her face seem like that of the statue of a stern, despairing goddess.

'My friend,' she said, in a low, firm tone, 'I appeal to you as the one only friend who could help me at this pass as I want to be helped. The help I ask from you I could not ask from Gertrude.'

'What is there that I would not do for you?'

'Perhaps you will not do this for me, but I do so hope and so trust that you will.'

'Tell me! tell me!' Jim said breathlessly.

'Well, you know as well as I do, you believe as well as I do, that life—mere life —life—life is not a great thing—is not the only thing—life without love, and the sense of honour and purity. Oh, you must understand!'

And Jim began to understand.

'Then,' she went on, 'will you bring me, when you come to-morrow—at ten o'clock, wasn't it?—a strong, sharp dagger? I shouldn't be able to make any use of the common or garden knife of commerce,' she said with another wan smile. 'It would bend, or break, or something, and I want to be quite, quite sure. Bring me a sharp, strong dagger with a keen point and a broadening blade. I promise you that it

shall only be used in the very, very last
resort; but I want to use it effectively
then. You will do this for me—you will
not refuse? You must understand the
feelings of a woman—the horror, the
loathing! You will do this for me '—and
her voice sank into an exquisite sweetness
and plaintiveness of tone—' my friend—in
this my very only friend?'

Jim had a moment of bewildering doubt
and agony. Then he said firmly :

' I will do this. That man shall not
get hold of you. Better go to your God.'

' Thank you,' she said fervently, and she
pressed his hand. ' And one thing more:
If the worst should happen, or the better
—if, anyhow, poor Gertrude should be
left alone—you will turn your thoughts to
her, will you not ?—will you not ?'

She did not wait for an answer—for an
answer which Conrad could not have
given—but she turned away, and ran out
of the room.

In a moment Gertrude entered.

'I don't want to keep you long,' she said, with a certain vague suggestion of scorn in her voice ; 'but I want you to do one thing for me, and not to tell anybody of it. I want you to buy me a good, small revolver, and come here at half-past nine to-morrow, and explain it all to me, and show me how to use it, and then load it for me.'

'What on earth do you want a revolver for ?' Jim asked, with a quite involuntary emphasis on the 'you.' The thought in his mind was, 'You are safe enough. Francis Rose does not propose to carry you off.'

'I want it to defend Clelia. If that wretch tries to carry her off I will shoot him !'

'Oh! I wouldn't do that,' Jim remonstrated. 'It would be absurd.'

'All right,' she said, with scornful eyes ; 'I can buy it for myself. There is a gun-

smith's in this street, only a few doors off.
I noticed it to-day. But I thought a man
might be of some use to one—only, I
suppose, he can't be. Well, we can do
without him—some of us, at all events.'

Jim was bewildered. Clelia's request
was tragic; Gertrude's bordered terribly on
the comic.

' Would they sell the girl a revolver ?'
he asked of himself. ' Yes, I suppose they
would. I'd better see that she gets a safe
little weapon that won't burst in her hands
on the first go-off.' He remembered in
his boyish days having bought a little
Derringer in a London shop after long
scraping up of pocket-money, and how, at
the very first pulling of the trigger, the
Derringer simply burst, and a fragment of
the barrel's metal lodged in his right hand,
and could not be got out for weeks after.
' That is the sort of weapon she would be
sure to buy,' he thought—' only with five
or six chambers to increase the danger.'

'Well?' she asked impatiently.

'All right,' he answered, 'or all wrong —I don't know which—I'll bring you the revolver to-morrow.'

'Thank you, and good-night.'

In a moment he was alone, and he went down the stairs and got into the hall, and passed out into the street, hardly knowing where he was or what he was doing. He had engaged to supply two young women with deadly weapons—one to commit suicide, the other to kill an enemy. His mind was completely topsy-turvy. Was the genteel, elegant, commonplace Albemarle Street hotel about to become a sort of Front de Bœuf's castle? And he knew that both the women from whom he had just parted were absolutely in earnest.

'Very well,' he said to himself, 'the laws can't help us. Some of us have only to act as the outlaw acts.'

The hotel stood not far from the opening of Grafton Street. As Jim turned into Grafton Street, he suddenly came in the moonlight on Sir Francis Rose's acquaintance, Captain Martin, the Patagonian traveller, who was so curiously modest, and even reticent, about his experiences in Patagonia. The meeting did not impress Jim at the time, but he remembered it afterwards. They exchanged a salutation hurriedly, and Jim passed through Grafton Street, and then wandered vaguely down Bond Street to Piccadilly. He was uncertain what to do. He would have liked to stand guard over Clelia's hotel all night long. He did, in fact, come back to the spot again and again. Hour after hour he revisited the scene, never leaving interval long enough for any complicated series of incidents to take place in the meantime.

At last it became to his mind quite clear that nothing was likely to happen that night, and he knew he had many things to think out before he was to return there next day, and so he went home.

Meanwhile the gallant Captain Martin had gone straight on to the Voyagers' Club and asked for Sir Francis Rose. Sir Francis Rose, it seemed, had left the club long before. Then Captain Martin went to the street near Berkeley Square, and found that the lights in his patron's flat were out. He thought that perhaps Sir Francis had not yet returned, and so he lingered longer—lingered very much longer; but at last he gave it up for that night. Sir Francis must have gone to bed, and it certainly was not worth disturbing him merely to tell him that Mr. Conrad had paid a late visit that night to the hotel in Albemarle Street.

'To-morrow will do,' he said.

CHAPTER XXV.

WHAT IS TO BE DONE NEXT?

JIM CONRAD thought it out that night with every fibre of his brain active and strained in the business of thinking. He wanted to prepare against all the difficulties—to stop all the earths, in the foxhunter's phrase. He felt sure at last that he had a plan as near to perfection as might be, in readiness for the morning's meeting. This was the outline of his plan : Clelia and Gertrude were to go to New York from Southampton ; they had been thinking and talking of going to the United States, and they might as well go now. The steamers that sail from Liverpool touch nearly all at Queenstown, and if Sir Francis Rose got a hint of his wife's having left from Liverpool, he would be waiting for her and ready to board the steamer at Queenstown; but the steamers sailing from Southampton make for the Atlantic straightway, and have no port to touch at.

There were many advantages, Conrad thought, in Clelia's going to New York. If once she got safely off, and by one of the fast steamers, there could be no possible pursuit for some days to come. Pursuit to the Continent is a matter merely of hours.

Then, Conrad did not believe that in New York the judicial authorities would be apt to trouble themselves much with intervention merely because an English married lady, whose husband did not profess to have any charge against her, had made a voyage to New York with another lady, even without his permission.

Jim's idea, therefore, was that he should

call at the Albemarle Street hotel early, bringing his sheaves with him—that is, his revolver and his dagger—for distribution, that he should divulge his whole scheme to the young women, and that, if they acceded to it, he should at once take berths for them in the first steamer sailing from Southampton. This day was Thursday, and the next steamer would leave Southampton at noon on the Saturday. That was coming to close quarters indeed; but, then, there were two lines of first-class steamers running every Saturday between Southampton and New York, and it was not a time of the year when Europeans rush across the Atlantic. Excepting for the depth of the winter, the early spring is perhaps the time when the Englishman has least idea or opportunity of undertaking a trip to America; therefore, Conrad had little doubt that he should be able one way or another to secure berths for Clelia and Gertrude and their maids.

Meanwhile, he thought the best thing to do would be to take rooms for them at one of the great hotels near to Westminster Bridge, and, by consequence, to the Waterloo Station—this end, if we may put it so, of Southampton.

He had thought first of a small hotel or of quiet lodgings in one of the narrow streets running off the Strand down to the river. But on turning the matter over in his mind he came to the conclusion that the safest thing of all would be to go to one of the great big flaring, crowded hotels of the Northumberland Avenue quarter. No one would be likely to assume that two women seeking escape from London would even for a single night domicile themselves in one of these vast open public places. He would go and take berths in the steamer—he would go and take rooms in the hotel; and later on the maids could quietly convey the luggage to the right place. But in the meanwhile Clelia and Gertrude would have to be left alone, and he could not bear the idea of leaving them at the Albemarle Street Hotel until he had arranged everything for their flight. Sir Francis would be almost certain to go to Albemarle Street that day and seek his wife.

What was to be done? Conrad racked his brain, and at last worked out an idea. He had thought of bestowing the young women in the National Gallery—'No one ever goes to the National Gallery,' he said to himself. No—he suddenly pulled up— that might be a reasonable description of things in general; but suppose anybody did go to the National Gallery, or suppose anybody were seen going into the National Gallery—suppose anybody were followed into the National Gallery—what protection would be afforded there for the pursued? The officials would simply bundle all the disputants into the street, and Sir

Francis would have a good chance of
securing his end. Jim had got to another
and a better idea. He would deposit the
ladies in the gallery of one of the courts
of law in the Strand, and let them wait
there until he had arranged all about the
passages and the hotel. Suppose Sir
Francis Rose, by an extraordinary possibility, were to find out that his wife was
in the gallery of one of the courts of law
—and supposing that anybody, not being
a practising lawyer there, could find his
way into any of the courts of law—and
suppose he were then and there to claim
his wife, and insist on carrying her off by
force, what would happen to him? The
judge, if he condescended to interrupt
public business by listening to his appeal,
and did not at once order him to be turned
into the street, would simply tell him that
he must proceed to enforce his rights by
the ordinary legal process, and then, if he
persevered in his interruption, would com-

mit him to prison for contempt of court.
All things considered, Jim Conrad came
to the conclusion that there was no sanc-
tuary in the world so absolutely safe in its
protection as the shelter of one of the law
courts in the Strand.　Jim could not help
thinking, amid all his excitement and his
frank recognition of the possibility of some
terrible tragedy being close at hand, that
the shelter in the law court was something
fit to suggest a scene to Mr. Gilbert.

He was up early; he had hardly slept
all night, his mind had been so engrossed
by his plans, and by the whole crisis, and
by the all but certainty that he was
soon to see Clelia for the last time.　Come
what would, it was all over between him
and her.　He had promised her that,
should she get off free, he would never
make any attempt to see her again.　He
would keep his word.　For the moment
he did not allow himself much time to
think over even this.　The effort to help

her sustained him. The hour had not come for thinking of his own hopeless love. That would come later on; there would be plenty of time for it when she had gone. What was he to do with himself when all that dream was over, and there remained nothing for him but the cold and crude and cruel routine and realities of daily life? Yet it is due to him to say that such were not the thoughts now uppermost in his mind. He was thinking only of how he might be most serviceable to her. He had got into that exalted frame of mind, that noblest of manly moods, whether it concerns a cause or a woman, when the man says to himself, and feels what he says: 'Let me perish, so it be well with you.'

He was with the young women in good time, and before he saw Clelia he gave Gertrude her revolver, and likewise a careful instruction in the use of it—a lesson which he directed rather with a view to her own personal safety than to any effective attack upon an enemy. Gertrude was very proud of the weapon and the instruction, and said that now at last she felt like a man. Conrad thought that if she felt like one particular man her feelings were by no means to be envied ; but he forbore from uttering his sentiments on that point. Both Clelia and Gertrude accepted his plans quite cordially. Clelia was just as willing to go to New York as to Paris, and, indeed, saw all the advantages that Jim eagerly pointed out. The rest was easy. The maids were to remain in Albemarle Street until Jim had taken berths in the steamer and rooms in the hotel, and came back and told them so. Then they were to carry the luggage to the hotel for which he had arranged. Meanwhile Clelia and Gertrude were to spend a delightful afternoon in one of her Majesty's Courts of Justice in the Strand, and to wait there until Jim should come to release them, and to consign them to the shelter of the Northumberland Avenue hotel.

The plan worked very smoothly. Clelia and Gertrude had the advantage of hearing the trial of a very important action which was brought to recover damages for injuries caused to the wife of the plaintiff by the servant of an omnibus company who had allowed his omnibus to knock her down in Old Broad Street, City. The court was not crowded, and there was plenty of room for the ladies in the gallery, where Jim had bestowed them. They did not give an absorbing attention to the case. They talked in low whispers to each other about matters of more immediate personal interest. Even the verdict of the jury failed to awaken them to any strong emotion— especially, perhaps, as neither of them had the least idea about which way the verdict went. Their thoughts were filled with Conrad's coming back; with the news he would bring them; with the chances of

their getting off to New York; with the
chances of their getting out of London un-
discovered and unmolested by Sir Francis
Rose. The time did not even seem to
hang upon their hands. We too com-
monly make up our minds to the belief
that hours of anxiety are necessarily slow
in their passing. There is an anxiety
which sometimes compresses and condenses
time.

Meanwhile the hours that Clelia and
Gertrude lingered and whispered through
in her Majesty's court of law in the
Strand were well employed by Jim Conrad
in driving round to the offices of steamship
companies and to big Northumberland
Avenue hotels. He was lucky enough to
secure berths in one of the steamers leaving
Southampton on Saturday—the very next
day—and his heart thrilled with his
success. Only think of it! The poor
youth was in love with Clelia Rose, and
yet his heart thrilled with the success

which took her away from him—in all
probability for ever. Love is cruelly
selfish sometimes, but sometimes, too,
Heaven be praised ! it is utterly unselfish.
' I have saved her,' Jim Conrad thought;
and for the moment that was all he
thought about.

He took rooms at one of the big hotels
—that was easy work. Then he drove
back to Albemarle Street and packed off
the maids. Nothing had been heard, he
knew by negative evidence, of Sir Francis
Rose. When the maids and the luggage
were off the premises, he stood for half a
moment at the door of the hotel. Just at
that half-moment, to his surprise, Captain
Martin happened to be passing by. They
exchanged a salute. This time the en-
counter set Jim thinking, but he could
make nothing of it.

Then he went back to the law court in
the Strand, and he set forth to the ladies what
he had done, and gave them their steamer

tickets, and told them about the hotel, and put them into a cab, and all was over.

Captain Martin had been looking for his patron early that morning, but had failed to find him. Sir Francis Rose had not been home all night. Captain Martin, not knowing anything better to do, had strolled up to Albemarle Street again later on, and there he saw Jim Conrad standing at the door. He went back again and again to the flat out of Berkeley Square, and at last, and when the day was pretty far advanced, he succeeded in seeing Sir Francis Rose, who had just come in from a revel at a fast country house some twenty miles from London, where he had been playing deeply and winning largely. The smile of a winner's exultation passed off Rose's features when he heard the news that Captain Martin had to tell.

'Why didn't you tell me this before?' he asked, in all the blind mechanical rage

of a man who wants to be furious with
somebody, and forgets that he himself is
alone to blame.

'Because I couldn't find you,' was the
answer, given politely, but with a certain
tone of injured dignity. 'You weren't
at home, and you didn't tell me where
you were going, or how I could com-
municate with you.'

'There's something in that,' Rose
admitted blandly, sadly. 'How very like
me to do such a thing as that! Well,
we must go to Albemarle Street at once;
and you, my esteemed and gallant friend,
must go in your capacity of detective
officer, accompanying me, and not as a
soldier and a Patagonian explorer.'

For all his fierce, impassioned fury
against Conrad, Rose began to see a
certain element of humour in the situation.

It is needless to say that they came
too late. The ladies had gone, and had

left no address. Nobody knew where
they had gone to. It was no affair of
the manager of the hotel. One of the
ladies might be the wife of the gentleman. The manager neither accepted nor
disputed the statement; but the names
in the hotel books were not those of
married ladies. The manager, in fact,
was totally indifferent, and did not seem
to care a button when he was informed
that one of those who called on him was
a detective officer. Sir Francis Rose
stormed a good deal at first, but then
became gradually impressed with the conviction that he was making a fool of himself. So he left the hotel and stalked out
into the evening air of Albemarle Street.
Then he put the police part of the in-
vestigation into the hands of the gallant
Captain Martin, especially enjoining him
to have the Dover and Folkestone steamers
looked after, and, of course, not to make
any row, but to see where the ladies were

going, if he could get at them. Rose
gave all these directions with an increasing conviction that Martin would be sure
to go to the wrong place and do the
wrong thing. Martin suggested that it
might be well to make inquiries at all
the big London hotels. Sir Francis Rose
smiled compassionately.

'Just like a professional detective,' he
said. 'As if there was the least chance
of their going to one of the big hotels!
But try there if you like.'

The professional pride of the detective
was offended, and he did not try.

Sir Francis rushed back to his flat. He
was in a mood of storm, and he blew up
the waves of the storm as a malign sea-god
might do who was determined on some act
of destruction. He sent a messenger at
once for Coffin. He was furious with
Coffin because nothing had been done.
Why had not Coffin carried out his promise
—his pledge? Did he expect to get the

house in the Rue de la Paix for nothing ? Did Coffin believe that he, Rose, was a fool ?—a 'blind buzzard idol,' as Milton says ? The idea and the words came into Rose's mind. He had read them in some quotation from Milton's prose writings long and long ago, and they had not flashed back upon his memory until now. 'Do they all believe I am a blind buzzard idol?' he savagely asked himself. 'Does Waley ? Does that sham Sir Galahad—that self-constituted squire of dames, Jim Conrad, believe it ? Does Clelia believe it ?' He would soon let them know—let them all and every one know—how confoundedly they were mistaken.

He looked at his watch ; for amid all his storming he remembered that he had arranged a pleasant little dinner-party at the Savoy Restaurant, and he was not going to be put off that by anybody. It was now seven o'clock.

Then he heard the electric bell at his

outer door tingle, and then there was a quick knock at his study door, and he shouted 'Come in,' and Marmaduke Coffin crept into the room with the familiar stealthiness of tread, and with a countenance of composed and self-satisfied gloom.

' So you have done nothing,' Rose said fiercely.

' Couldn't do anything. Hadn't a chance.'

' My Heaven !' Rose exclaimed, ' I am well off between you. Waley can't get this young fellow even to leave the country, and you can't get him——'

' Out of the world,' said Coffin grimly.

' Out of the world—yes, if you like to put it in that way,' Rose answered, with a contemptuous toss of his head.

' Put it any way you like, chief,' said the imperturbable Coffin.

' I suppose I must take it in hand my-self,' Rose said with increasing scorn, for he began to be afraid that both his retainers were cooling in their ardour for his cause.

'Good idea!' Coffin said, nodding with an air of grave approval—something like that which an undertaker might assume as he accepted a suggestion about the arrangement of the hearse.

'What do you mean by a good idea?'

'Idea of your going into the thing yourself. Go to his house, lodging, whatever it is, demand to know about your wife, talk up and loud. Quarrel follows—I'll take care of him in quarrel. Judicial inquiry—injured husband seeking lawful wife—row—attack on injured husband—faithful friend, too zealous, defends him—assailant killed — nothing planned — no murder—all parties get easily off. Injured husband leaves court without stain on character—zealous friend gets twelve months at most—and then house Rue de la Paix!'

'By Jove! I think there's something in

what you say,' Rose declared, and his eyes sparkled with cruel satisfaction. He had always felt a little doubtful about the consequences to himself in case he should secure the assassination of Conrad. In his present mood of hatred and revenge he would not have been deterred by any such consideration—that is, he would not have held back the murderous hand.

Still, it might be a very serious business for him, and even if he should get out of the country all right, it would perhaps involve questions of extradition and all that troublesome sort of thing, allowing a traveller no rest anywhere for the sole of his foot. He thought there was a stroke of positive genius in Coffin's suggestion.

'Thou art the best of the cut-throats !' he exclaimed.

'Am I really ?' Coffin asked, quite gratified.

'I was only quoting from Shakespeare,' Rose added hurriedly.

'Indeed,' said Coffin placidly; 'I never read Shakespeare. I saw a play of his once in Paris—I don't remember where, and I forget what it was.'

Then he shut his mouth.

Rose strode up and down the room, thinking the whole thing right out. He had not in his mind the slightest suspicion as to the integrity of his wife. Neither when he loved her madly, as he did once before, and as he did now, or when he hated her madly, as he had done before, did he ever fail to recognise the genuine purity of her nature. But he hated Conrad none the less.

There was a pause. Rose looked at Coffin as if he expected him to say something oracular. Coffin was equal to the occasion. The oracle spoke.

'Send for Waley,' Coffin said.

'What in the name of patience do we want with Waley?' Rose asked angrily.

He was for the moment quite disappointed with the oracle.

'Waley will go to help you in recovering your wife. Waley no man of violence. Good witness, Waley—show that it was all only a row—no plan—no thought of killing anyone.'

'By Jove! you are right again,' Rose exclaimed. 'Coffin, you positively shine to-night. You may count on that house in the Rue de la Paix, provided, of course, you get the job done.'

'Leave the job to me. You pitch into Conrad pretty hard, threaten him, make him attack you—mind, make him attack you. Leave the rest to me. We'll call Waley as evidence.'

'Go for Waley at once,' Rose said.

'No. Better you wire for Waley yourself.'

'Why so?'

'Better. Will please him to be sent for by you. Thinks, perhaps, he is left too

much out of the business—inner circle,
you know. Send for him and consult him
—make it all right.'

'What put that idea into your head?'
Rose asked sharply.

'Have a head—idea got into it—that's
all.'

'Yes, you have a head,' Rose said in a tone
of admiration. 'I am sure you are right
in this, too. I'll wire for Waley at once.'

'I'll take the wire,' Coffin said.

'Why so? I can send it by the
messenger.'

'Better I should take it.'

'For what reason? They might know
you at the post-office.'

'All right. That's it.'

'That's what?'

'I take a message asking the man who
is not violent to come with us. Shows
there is no plan for killing prepared by
anyone. See?'

Sir Francis's features relaxed into a

smile for the first time that evening. He
was beginning to wonder how he had
failed to see Coffin's striking qualities so
long. He wrote the message asking
Waley to come to him at half-past eleven
—for he meant to enjoy his dinner—and
handed it to Coffin for delivery; and then
alone he waited in some anxiety—not as
to what was to be done—for about that
his determination did not falter—but about
the manner of doing it.

He did not believe for a moment that
Conrad had any plan for carrying off his
wife. He knew perfectly well that
nothing of the kind had ever entered into
Conrad's head, and he was equally sure
that had it entered there, it would have
had to pass out again quite unfulfilled.
But he felt none the less hatred to Conrad
on that account. The conviction was
settled deep down in his heart that but for
Conrad he should have got his wife again
—with her money.

The little dinner - party was very pleasant, and Rose left it reluctantly. His weakness was that he never at any given moment quite knew which enjoyment he preferred. He went home and met Waley, and told his story.

'Don't believe a word of it,' Waley quickly answered. 'What I mean is that I am quite sure you are misinformed, chief. I know the young chap pretty well. I can size up any man when I come to study him, and I don't believe he ever thought of doing anything of the sort.'

'You seem to have a high opinion of him, Waley,' Rose said with passionate contempt in his look and his voice.

'So I have.'

'Well, at any rate, your impeccable friend has been helping my wife to get away from me——'

'That's quite another pair of shoes, don't you see? A man might do the one thing who wouldn't do the other.'

'Do you dare to back him up, Waley—here, to my face?'

'I don't back him up. I believe a man ought to be very careful how he interferes between husbands and wives, anyhow—I suppose that is religion, ain't it? But there are degrees in wrong-doing, I take it for granted.'

'The man who interferes between me and my wife shall pay the penalty for it,' Rose exclaimed.

'Quite right,' came in the raven voice of Coffin, who had been with Rose before Waley arrived.

'Let it be so,' Waley said. 'What do you propose to do?'

'I'll go to his rooms, and I'll talk to him, and he must tell me where my wife has gone, or I'll know the reason why.'

'Suppose he doesn't know?' Waley asked in perfect good faith.

'Oh, rot! He does know. I have

evidence that he was there this very day, and late last evening also.'

'Suppose he won't tell?'

'He shall tell. I'll drag the story from his very throat!'

'Well, do you want me to go with you on this expedition?'

'Yes; I think you ought to be with me. I think you ought to stand by and help me. Are you my friend, or are you my enemy?'

'I am your friend, chief, and not your enemy, as you know well; and just because I am your friend I'll go with you on this business. Who else is going? You don't want a crowd, I suppose?'

'Coffin is going,' Rose said, not without a certain visible reluctance and a scrutinizing look at Waley's face.

'Oh, Coffin's going? All right. Yes, I'll go, certainly. But I should have thought two to one would be enough for all purposes.'

'How do I know what confounded devil's work such a scoundrel may be up to ?'

'Oh, you take it in that way ! Very well, I'm with you, chief. I can see fair play, at all events, if I can do nothing else.'

Rose cast a keen, distrustful glance at him, but said nothing.

'When shall we go ?' Waley asked.

Rose answered :

'Now.'

CHAPTER XXVI.

A LEAP IN THE DARK.

JIM CONRAD returned late to his home in Clarges Street. His long day's work was done. He had taken leave of his friends. He had made every arrangement for them, and he was to see them no more. They were all agreed that he must not see them off by the train for Southampton, and that they were to go their way alone. Clelia, he knew, would not write to him—at least, for a long time.

It could hardly be said that the sacrifice was consummated, for in his case there was no sacrifice to consummate. Clelia was a married woman, and a pure woman, and there was nothing for him to sacrifice ; he had nothing to give up which could have been his, which he could have held. But he felt like one who had lost all that makes life dear. He looked mournfully, pathetically, and yet with a certain grim sense of the ludicrous, at the fitting-up of the rooms in which he had taken so much pride and pleasure, while yet it was not all certain—not all quite certain—that his hopes and his love must be blighted. He sat down and smoked a cigar, and glanced at the books and the pictures, the etchings and the colour-sketches, which had once been a delight to him to arrange in their places.

The one desire—the immemorial desire —of the young man whose love is made hopeless was borne in strongly on him. He had now no thought but for the consolation of going away—of travelling far and wide ; of drenching and drowning his grief in years of wandering. Some lines of a great and now all-but-forgotten

poet came into his mind—lines that he
had not seen or thought of since he was a
romantic boy, and he felt their force with
a thrilling intensity :

> 'I care not to what land ye bear,
>   So not again to mine.'

'Now is the time for Waley and
Patagonia,' he muttered to himself. 'Now
let Waley arrange for me what plans he
will in Patagonia. Patagonia is not by
any means too far away for me. I should
like to go to the land east of the sun, west
of the moon,' and he thus came in his
poetic rhapsody to a more modern poet
than the author of 'Childe Harold.'

It was late—wellnigh on to midnight.
He was roused by a sharp and reiterated
ring at the electric bell in the hall-door.
He felt sure that the servants were all in
bed, and, as it so happened, he was now the
only lodger in the house. He ran quietly
downstairs and opened the door, at which,

even as he stood there, another pressure
sent the bell tingling once again through
the house, and he could hear a voice out-
side which seemed to be speaking in re-
monstrance against the hastily repeated
summons.   Jim undid the bolts and the
chain, opened the door, and saw, in the
soft moonlight, three men standing on the
pavement.   The whole purpose was made
clear to him when he heard the voice of
Sir Francis Rose.

'I have come to know what you
have done with my wife!' Rose asked
fiercely.

Even in that note the voice sounded
strangely musical.

Conrad's courage and composure came
back to him in a moment.   He was not
much surprised, after all.   Something like
this was to be expected ; the wonder was
that he had not expected it.

'If you will come in, and come upstairs, Sir Francis Rose,' he said very

quietly, 'I shall be quite ready to give you any explanation that it is in my power to give.'

'All right! all right!' the cheery voice of Waley came in. 'That is just what we want to have. Come in, chief; we mustn't make a row. This sort of thing is best talked of quietly, and indoors.'

'Quite right! quite right!' sounded the deep funereal notes of the solemn Coffin.

The three came in, and Conrad closed the door. They mounted the stairs in absolute silence, and Conrad showed them into his room.

'It is a little late,' he said, 'and the house is quiet. There are only women-servants, and they are all in bed, and I don't want any noise made. But I am quite willing, Sir Francis Rose, to talk to you on any subject you wish to mention——'

'You've got to!' Coffin grumbled in.

'Shut up, Coffin!' Waley urged in a low tone.

'Where is my wife?' Rose demanded, striding quite closely up to Conrad, and looking him fiercely in the face.

'Easy now, easy!' said the peace-making Waley.

'Your wife is a lady for whom I have the deepest respect,' Jim answered calmly.

'Respect!   Confound your respect! Where is she?'

'That's the question,' Coffin said.

'Shut up, Coffin!' Waley again inter-posed.   'She isn't your wife, anyhow.'

'I cannot tell you where your wife is,' Jim replied.   'I know she is determined not to trust herself again to you.'

'You seem to know too much about her.'

'There are things one can't help know-ing.'

'You helped her to get away from me?'

'I did; and another friend, much closer and dearer to her—a woman.'

'I know—I thought so! You hear, Waley; you hear, Coffin?'

Waley merely nodded. Coffin groaned.

'Yes, I hear. Regular conspiracy, nothing else.'

'Shut up, Coffin!' Waley broke in.

'Will you fight me like a man?' Rose demanded of Jim.

'We don't fight duels in England nowadays,' Jim answered.

'Then, you are a coward?'

'I don't suppose I am any braver than other men. But I shouldn't be a coward if I wanted to kill you. I don't.'

'We don't fight duels in England nowadays!' Rose said scoffingly. 'You have been out of England, haven't you—in countries where men do fight duels?'

·'I have,' Jim answered gravely.

A thought had come up in his mind, and he was trying to turn it over.

'Will you come to Calais, or Boulogne, or Ostend?'

Jim had had his thought out.

'Yes,' he said.   'Whenever you like. To-morrow?'

'Come, that's all right; nothing can be fairer,' the considerate Waley remarked, anxious to bring the whole business to any sort of compromise, or close, if only for the night.

'But how about Lady Rose in the meantime?' croaked Coffin.

'Confound you!' Waley muttered.

Rose caught at the hint.

'Yes, what about my wife?' he demanded.   'You are right, Coffin.   What about her?   I see now the meaning of your sudden burst of courage.   I should be away at Boulogne or Ostend while your pals were enabling my wife to get away from me.   That's your dodge!'

'You have given the invitation; I accept it,' Jim said coldly.

' And a very fair thing,' Waley declared.

Then Rose found himself in a dilemma. He saw no way out of it for the moment but to lose his temper and throw the rest on fate. For the moment, too, he forgot the precise nature of his bargain with Coffin; or he saw no likelihood that Jim would give him a chance of having it carried out according to the conditions.

' You are a coward,' he exclaimed, ' and I couldn't fight with you ! I am a gentle-man, and not a sentimental trickster ! But I can chastise you, thank Heaven !'

He had a light cane in his hand, and he rushed on Jim and struck him across the face and shoulders. Jim gripped him with all his strength, and twisted the cane from his hands, and flung it across the room. Waley tried in vain to part the struggling men. Rose was tearing like a madman ; Jim was perfectly composed, and was only striving to ward off the attack. At last, when he had had too much of the struggle,

he gripped his arms round Rose's waist,
lifted him fairly off his feet, and threw
him across the room. Rose was dashed
against the opposite wall, and brought to
a stand there ; and there he fell, and there
he lay.

'Easy now,' Waley said, putting a re-
straining hand on Jim's chest. 'You're
not to blame ; but let him alone.'

'I didn't want to touch him, Waley,'
Jim replied angrily.

Then Coffin found himself confronted
with the most serious dilemma of his
recent career. He had based all his calcu-
lations on the understanding that Rose
would provoke Conrad to make an attack
on him. The moment this was done,
Coffin would plunge forwards to save the
life of his patron. Conrad was a younger
and much stronger man than Rose, and it
was not to be supposed that he, Coffin,
could exactly know how far Conrad might
not carry his murderous purpose. There-

fore, to save his friend and patron's life from what he might well believe to be an imminent danger, what could be more natural, more pardonable, and even more praiseworthy, than that he should rush in between, and make that life certain at any cost ?

'I shall get something for it,' he had always reasoned to himself, 'but what will it be ? Unpremeditated action—mere defence of my friend—six months—twelve months —that sort of thing. And then there is the house in the Rue de la Paix.'

But now behold how things had fallen out ! There was Rose the aggressor— Rose, who had clearly striven his best to harm Conrad—and there was Conrad, who had at last merely flung him off like a spatter, and was now standing composedly, and to all appearance with no desire to harm mortal man ! Alas ! how easily things go wrong !

Still, Coffin made up his mind that

something must be done for the money. He had no faith in the revolver; he had the true assassin's faith in the knife. He made up his mind. He drew his knife—he sprang on Conrad, and he screamed out:

'You murderer, you want to kill my friend!' and he brandished the knife on high.

But for Coffin's one moment of hesitation, excusable, no doubt, under the suddenly altered conditions, it would probably have been all over with Jim Conrad. For nothing could have been farther from Jim's thought than to suppose that anybody except perhaps Sir Francis Rose really wanted to kill him. Therefore, he was not standing on his guard, and was not thinking about any manner of personal danger. He was only hoping that he had not done Sir Francis any serious harm in the heavy fall which he could not help giving him. But Coffin's one moment of consideration had been the ruin of Coffin's plan, for it gave Waley time to be on the watch, and to understand the situation. Just as the knife was raised he seized Coffin by the back of the collar, and dragged him away with a strength which Coffin found it hopeless to resist. He flung Coffin on the floor, and clutched both of his wrists with a tremendous grip.

' Quick, quick !' he called to Jim ; ' take the knife from him and open the window and call for the police.'

Rose was still lying on the floor, either stunned by the sharp fall or not caring to rise until something definite should happen.

Waley was holding Coffin down by main strength. Suddenly an alarmed tapping of various sets of knuckles was heard at the door.

' Tell the servants they have no business here,' Waley called to Jim. ' Let them send quietly for the police. You and I can hold these two here until they come.'

'No, no, no police!' Jim called out.

He was thinking of Clelia's name dragged into an ignoble quarrel.

Jim opened the door and had a confused vision of the landlady and some other women, who had evidently got out of bed 'just as they were,' to adopt a way of expressing it which they would probably have used, and he quietly told them that there was no further danger, and that they might go to bed again.

Meanwhile, Rose had staggered to his feet. He was pale to ghastliness; he saw that the whole scheme was a failure, and that it was his own hasty action which had made the failure complete. His hate was now turned from Conrad to Coffin; he hated Coffin all the more because he had himself given to Coffin the reason for his moment of delay in decisive action.

'Let him get up, Waley,' Rose said imperiously. 'We don't want any police ferreting into all this business. Let him

get up, I tell you, and let him go away.
Mr. Conrad and I can settle any accounts
we have to settle in our own way, without
the help of you, or of Coffin, or of the
police.'

'I have no accounts to settle,' Jim said
contemptuously. 'If any man attacks me
in front I shall take good care of myself,
and perhaps he may not be altogether glad
of his attempt. I could have done so just
now if I had suspected anything. I don't
want the police any more than Sir Francis
Rose does.'

'You had better let me get up,' Coffin
called out, struggling with his legs on the
floor, and striving with all his might and
main to lift Waley from off his chest.

He could not manage it, however.

'Let him get up, Waley,' Jim said; 'let
us have an end of all this one way or
another.'

'Have you got the knife?' Waley asked
eagerly.

'Yes, I've got the knife safe enough. Let him get up.'

Waley rose to his feet.

'Get up, you murdering ruffian!' he said.

And in rising he gave Coffin a contemptuous touch of his foot.

'I don't want to do anybody any harm,' Coffin murmured, with bated breath. 'Thought that chap was going to kill my friend—lost my temper, that's all.'

'Your friend, you infernal bungling coward!' Rose cried. 'You don't want to do anyone any harm? No, of course you don't. Take that!'

And he struck Coffin a violent blow on the face.

Coffin saw that the game was up, so far as he was concerned; the chance of the house in the Rue de la Paix was utterly gone. He was seized with all the fury of despair.

'Look here, Mr. Conrad and Mr.

Waley,' he exclaimed, 'that man who has hit me—that man engaged me to kill Mr. Conrad! It's a put-up job, I tell you. Let him deny it if he dares.'

Rose endeavoured to strike at him again, but Waley threw his stalwart form between them, and held Rose off. Rose mastered himself once again. He turned away with a swagger, and said:

'You all appear to be such good friends that I don't seem as if I ought to intrude on so charming a comradeship any longer. I shall recover my wife in spite of you all. Good-night, gentlemen!'

Then he turned and left the room, and they heard him moving to the stairs. But there was a noise below, of heavy footsteps.

'By Jove! they have sent for the police,' Waley said. 'They were right, and I'm awfully glad of it.'

Rose came rushing back into the room. Before any of them could guess what he meant to do, he had thrown up the window.

'I am not going to be caught in your infernal trap,' he cried ; and he strode into the balcony, climbed over the railing, and dropped into the street below. Conrad and Waley ran to the window ; Coffin remained where he was, wholly impassive now. A heavy fall was heard, and then a faint, low moaning. Rose had evidently in his passion miscalculated the depth of the descent. No sound of flying feet was heard, only the low moaning, like that of some stunned and wounded animal.

'I'm afraid he has done for himself now,' Waley said, with a deep note of pity and of grief in his voice.

'I am afraid he has,' Jim echoed ; and there was horror in his heart.

'Serve him right !' growled the funereal voice of Coffin. 'Why did he break his bargain ?'

Then the police came in, and there were a few rapid words of explanation ; and Jim and Waley went down to the street with the officers.   Sir Francis Rose was lying with his head and one arm terribly fractured.   He had evidently cannoned against something in his fall, and come head downwards on to the pavement.

CHAPTER XXVII.

THE long anxious hours of the night wore themselves away. Rose had been carefully lifted up, and tenderly carried to Jim's room and stretched upon Jim's bed. A doctor and a surgeon were sent for. Both agreed that Rose could not then be removed to his own home or to any hospital. Both seemed to be of opinion that there would be no need of any intermediate removal. Rose had been terribly injured on the head.

The police soon left the place, having taken the names of all those present with a view to a probable inquest. Mr. Coffin, having given his name, had quietly left the sitting-room and descended the stairs and disappeared, never to appear again, so far as this story is concerned. Jim and Waley both 'spotted' him, to use Waley's phrase, as he was making off; neither had the faintest idea of detaining him. To what end should he be detained ? The less said about the whole tragedy the better. Jim was thinking of Clelia ; Waley was thinking of the chief, for whom he once had such admiration——for whom he had still so much regret.

For a long time Rose was insensible. He merely kept moaning on; but for the moaning, the listeners could hardly have known whether he was alive or dead. The surgeon found that his brain was pressed upon by a fragment of bone, and after a while a successful operation relieved the patient from that oppression, and he recovered his senses, and even his spirits, and he made inquiry about himself in quite a cheery sort of way :

'A question of days, doctor, or a question of hours?'

'A question of hours, I am afraid.'

'Well,' he murmured in a low tone, 'one must die at one hour or another. Odd how true it is, that old story, that nobody ever believes it of himself! I never believed that anything could kill me; now I tumble off a balcony by mere accident, and, lo and behold! I kill myself.'

Even then Rose had his wits about him enough to do his best to set the belief going that his impending death was but the result of a commonplace sort of accident.

The morning came, first pallid and then roseate. Meanwhile, at the urgent recommendation of Jim Conrad, the doctor— whose close services were not then needed —had gone to seek Lady Rose. He took with him a few lines from Conrad, simply asking her to put herself in the hands of the doctor, and announcing that Sir

Francis was lying dangerously ill. It was agreed among them all that the doctor was the best messenger who could be charged with such an errand, and he was quite willing to undertake the mission.

About eight o'clock Rose turned to the surgeon, who was alone in the room with him, and quietly said:

'I have an odd fancy—I should like to see my wife, Lady Rose. I don't know where she is just now, but I dare say Mr. Conrad could tell you.'

'I know where she is,' was the quiet answer.

'You do—yes? Where is she?'

'She is here.'

And in a moment he had left the room, and Clelia had entered it, and was standing by the bed.

'Come near me, Clelia,' he whispered; 'come nearer—nearer—quite near.'

She drew close to him, and bent over him, her heart beating, the tears standing

in her eyes.   The end was coming.   She
felt for a moment as if it might be the end
of the world.

'Clelia, do you forgive me—do you
forgive me all?'

The whole past came back upon her.
In   the   sudden   light   of   consciousness
illumined by that flash of memory, she
saw   her   girlhood   and   her   youth—her
hero-worship and her strong love.   And
there beneath her, just about to die, was
her first love and her husband.   All the
wrong, the quarrel, the stain, the shame,
passed out of her mind, and she could
only remember Francis Rose as her first
love and the husband of her youth.

'Oh, Francisco!' she murmured, 'God
knows how truly I forgive you!   Oh, I
forgive you with all my heart, and with
all my soul and all my strength.   Forgive
you! forgive you!'

And she stooped down and kissed him
on the forehead, compassionately, tenderly.

He turned as if a little wearily.

'That's all right,' he said, cheerily enough. 'And I forgive you, Clelia.'

She drew back a little, shocked and pained. For with the forgiving words from him the memory of her wrongs came back to her. It is very sweet to be forgiven when one is conscious of having done wrong, but to be forgiven when one has strained the most generous faculties of one's nature is a little hard, even at a death-bed.

'You forgive me?' she asked — 'for what?'

And then she felt compunction for having put such a question to a dying man.

Sir Francis smiled a quiet, amused smile — distinctly amused, although he was dying. It was so like a woman, he thought, to put such a question.

'I forgive you, Clelia,' he said, 'for having been all through your life too good for me, and so making me think that we couldn't get on together. That's all I have to forgive you for; but it's a great deal, dear girl! for a bad lot like me. One gets tired of finding his wife always too good for him. Do you know, I was rather glad, on the whole, to find that you had enough of the world, and the flesh, and the devil in you to let that other fellow fall in love with you!'

She had been kneeling beside him. Now she rose up.

' Must we part like this?' she said. ' Oh, Frank! do not let us part like—like this.'

Then there was a pause. The current of his thoughts seemed to have changed. He spoke abruptly, his voice still quite clear :

' Don't you trouble about me, Clelia. The whole thing was my fault ; I know that well enough. But I couldn't help myself. And I'm not a bit sorry to be

going off. I have muddled things in this
world. So I want a new sensation. I
have got pretty well all that is to be got
out of this world, and, do you know, I am
greatly interested in the idea of some quite
new and fresh experience. I wonder what
it will be like ?'

'Oh, Frank,' she pleaded passionately,
'don't talk like that! Oh, don't, don't !
it's all so serious—so terrible.'

'Serious? terrible ? No, I don't think
so. Anyhow, I want to find out what it
is all about. I tell you, Clelia, I want
a new start. Don't you trouble about
me.'

'Oh !' she exclaimed under her breath,
and she tossed her head impatiently. She
strove that he should not see it, but she
could not help her impatience. To see
him meet death in this sort of spirit ! To
think that he could feel no more than
that ! Only a vague curiosity and a desire
for some manner of new sensation !

There was another pause.   Then he asked, in tones less·clear and more gasping than before :

'Clelia, did you ever get back that ring ?'

'Yes, Frank,' she said softly.

'He gave it to you ?'

'Yes—oh yes ; it was mine ; and, of course, when he knew that he gave it back to me.'

'Have you it now—with you here ?'

'Oh yes.'

'Would you mind giving it back to me, Clelia ?   I have a fancy that I should like to carry it with me—to put it out of your way for ever.   Then, you can forget, if you like, that I ever threw you away, and that you ever threw the poor old ring away, and so we are quits.   Do you see the idea ?'

She was not wearing the ring.   She had it in a little purse which she carried in her pocket.   She found the purse and took out the ring. It was a strange thought that came into her mind just then : the thought of how methodical it all was, how formal it was, how that which might have been strange and thrilling if one were to read it described in a novel seemed so much a matter of course here and now—between life and death.

She had given up all hope of prevailing on him to take death seriously. He could not, he would not—he was still acting a play.

'Oh,' she thought, with a rush of pity and compassion flooding through her heart, 'if, after all, that was his nature, if he could not help it, if play-acting throughout life was his doom and not his choice, then may that be to his account with the Power which will not misjudge him as I have misjudged him ! Ah, who made him a play-actor, after all ? and shall he not find pity and pardon ?'

So she put the ring upon his finger.

His eyes had been closed. He opened them and smiled.

'Suppose it turned out to be a talisman,' he said—'a kind of emblem of forgiveness? Well, anyhow, I'll take it with me—as far as I can. Oh, don't you cry, Clelia! I have had a good time in this world. I got almost everything I wanted, and now I leave you to have a good time. You can marry your friend.'

'Oh, for pity's sake,' she pleaded, 'don't say things like that.'

'Why not? Why shouldn't you marry him? He is awfully fond of you—I found out that—and I don't see why you should not be fond of him. I never gave you a fair chance of keeping on being fond of me. I don't mind your marrying him. Clelia, will you kiss me on the lips—on the lips?'

She stooped silently over him and kissed him.

'Do you know, Clelia, I felt that kiss

delightful. I think this is the most interesting hour to me of all our married life—yes, the most interesting by far. Wasn't there some great Roman who, when he was dying, said to his friends that he felt himself turning into a god?— wasn't there? wasn't there?'

He rolled his head upon the pillow, and looked eagerly into her dimming eyes with his eyes quick-glancing, and seeming to have a sudden ray of new life in them.

'I think there was. I don't know—I am not sure. Why should we think of such things now?'

'Because I feel so like all that. I am longing for the new experience—the other world; but it is a delight to linger just this moment with you. Come, I think you will admit that I am meeting death like a man, and a North-Country man. Will you kiss me again?'

She was bending her lips towards him, when he suddenly drew away.

'No,' he murmured faintly ; 'it would
only spoil the effect.   Such a sensation
could never be reproduced.   Once, and
once only, for a moment like that!   Nothing
now left but the other sensation—the
other quite new sensation—the world elsewhere !'

Then he turned his head slightly away,
and his eyes closed again.   A complete
silence reigned all around.   Clelia was as
much the victim of a new sensation as
any that could meet her husband in the far
world to which he was yearning to go.
She was terrified—horrified—by his way
of encountering death.   She had, even in
her limited experience, looked on death
before, but never on such a death as this—
never a death that was treated by the
dying mortal as a new and dramatic experience, as the curious and interesting
prelude to yet more strange, and perhaps
even more interesting experiences !

This was indeed a way of looking at

things which was shocking to a woman with the nature and the feelings of Clelia Vine. There was something ghastly, something that oppressed her with a sense of the unnatural, and even the diabolic, about it. She gazed on the face of the dying man as she might, in another age, have gazed on the face of one possessed by a demon — the face of one in whom any supernatural or subnatural transformation might be expected. And, meanwhile, the face of the dying man was, in its expression, calm, composed, and sweet as the placid countenance of a sinking saint.

There is not much left to tell. The inquest was held, and ended only in a verdict of 'Accidental death,' although it was described in the papers as 'The Clarges Street Mystery.' There had been a quarrel—blows were interchanged. The police had been brought in by the people of the house. Sir Francis Rose, dreading to have his family name mixed up in any such affair, had in a moment of impulse tried to get out by the window, and missed his mark and fallen on the pavement. All that happened was truly told, only the cause of the quarrel did not come out. It had, indeed, nothing to do with the question for the coroner's jury.

The passages taken for New York were merely transferred to another boat. Clelia and Gertrude went out to New York, and Gertrude concerned herself there and elsewhere in America with the cause of woman's true advancement. She carried the flag, with Clelia in the quiet background, out to San Francisco, and up to Lake Superior, and down to New Orleans and the Gulf of Mexico. Conrad did not see either of them before they left. It was understood that he should hear from them—some time.

Waley went abroad on some enterprise to South America. He pressed Conrad to go with him, but Conrad remained in Europe, and wandered about there aimlessly for a long time. He could not pull himself together all at once. He gave himself a loose rein and went his way, dreaming of brighter days to come—which days came.

He heard news of Clelia at last. Gertrude wrote to him, and then Clelia, too, wrote to him—and more than a year passed before they three met once again. They met at Venice, and there Jim and Clelia were married. Then Clelia and Jim proposed to travel slowly on to Egypt. Gertrude took leave of them bravely. She meant to return for awhile to the United States, where she seemed to see a wide sphere of influence opening before her.

'I ought to be very happy,' she said. 'Until now I have had only a sister, now I have a sister and a brother.'

She kissed Clelia fondly, and Clelia returned her kisses.

'Now,' murmured Clelia, her eyes glancing in tears, 'kiss your brother, Gertrude.'

And Gertrude put her arm timidly, tenderly, on Jim's shoulder, and drew him down to her and kissed him.

And Jim's novel? It will be finished, perhaps, some time. If not, the world will still go on—there are so many novels nowadays! But both Jim and Clelia are resolved that he shall not live a useless life —that he shall be 'not a shadow among shadows, but a man among men.'

THE END.

BILLING AND SONS, PRINTERS, GUILDFORD.

www.ingramcontent.com/pod-product-compliance
Lightning Source LLC
Chambersburg PA
CBHW030127030726
47498CB00007B/2583